C000245878

William The Conqueror

Ruarri Joseph is a musician, writer, husband and father. He lives in Newquay in the South West of England.

William The Conqueror is both his first novel and the name of the band in which he writes, sings and plays guitar.

Albums by William The Conqueror
Maverick Thinker (2021)
Bleeding On The Soundtrack (2019)
Proud Disturber of The Peace (2017)

Albums by Ruarri Joseph
Brother (2013)
Shoulder to the Wheel (2011)
Both Sides of the Coin (2009)
Tales of Grime and Grit (2007)

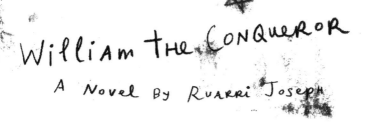

William the Conqueror

A Novel by Ruarri Joseph

First published by Blue Raincoat Books in 2021

ISBN: 978-1-8383455-0-1

To that kid.

1   31st DECEMBER, 1999.

LONDON, SE8

You've caught me at a bad time for sure. I took a real howler of a wrong turn somewhere, swallowed my tongue and covered my ears a long time ago. I'm twenty-four storeys high, suddenly scared. I opened the window and let the night's icy talons set my rubber body bristling. I couldn't face my reflection any more—gormless and gunning for his skin to shed, thinking he's the victim with those dinner-plate eyes and that song-less mouth too dry to drool. His straw-ginger hair hides a multitude of cradle cap. His Roman beak prickles at the nostrils that hoovered up the drugs so hungrily—another link in the chain of dumb choices. He looks like he threw up his lungs. Not exactly a role model.

What did you expect?

The city from here is a blanket of blimp burns and cheap jewellery, self-harmed with siren blue flecks in street-lit veins. It bleeds a frosty golden sap of false promise and I fell for it. Fuck you, London.

Let it all out.

The stars above me.

Careful now.

Glass shards sparkling in eternity. Incorruptible hopes in god's own wilderness. And the fireworks haven't even started.

> *I'll give you that, just for having the nuts to try. The stars are a tricky one. Overdone. Ripe for nauseating metaphor. I hope you used god with a small 'g'.*

When the first New Year rocket goes up I'll be nineteen, alone and undone.

> *Christ with a small 'c'!*

My mind is boiling.

> *Indeed.*

Once it'd been corridors of neatly stacked memories in a giant and welcoming library. I was the keeper of the keys and the infinite index. Now, it's a broth of bubbling slurry. White noise burning in a cauldron left to spill. I want to piece my life together, but everything's scattered like a crime scene in a hurricane. The truth blustered around in the nameless streets and then scarpered with the assailants. I'm the low-life deadbeat detective, scouring the nooks for clues long lost.

Listen man, Lionel Hutz nailed it when he said there's the truth—shakes head—and the truth—nods furiously! It's a perspective thing, see? Don't worry about it.

Forgive me.

Forgiven. Wait. What for? Who you talking to?

It's like I asked around for a smoke and missed the whole show. Ticket and head in hands as usual.

You took a risk.

I'm sorry.

Sorry enough.

Make a start. Where am I? How did I get here?

London. You waved your fob at the entrance and took the lift like always. You're living the dream in inverted commas, twenty-four storeys high.

Somewhere to go, but nowhere to be.

Sure.

What did I do?

Too much is all. First-time flyers aren't usually so hungry. They use that shit on horses, man.

3

I want to crawl out the window.

That's metaphor, right?

She remembered my name.

You're pretty hard to forget.

This needs to end now.

Some turbulence in the K-hole? A little altitude sickness maybe?

I want to see. Let it flash before my eyes.

It's not like you to want to look back. You've trespassed there before. It was a luckless fruit that fell on tar, remember? Nothing can come of it. Wait—are you praying?

Darkness at the break of noon.

Here we go again.

Shadows even the silver spoon.

You really want to go there?

The handmade blade, the child's balloon, eclipses both the sun and moon.

4

Okay. You win. Extenuating circumstances and all. Just don't go soft on me again. Perhaps step away from the window?

To understand you know too soon...

There is no sense in trying! Alright, fuck it! Rabbit holes don't dig themselves. Grab your shovel and off we go. Might as well do it properly and not skip bits. From the top. The very top. And a one, and a two, and a...

Midnight. London erupts before me.

It won't stick. It's cow shit to a ceiling fan but go ahead—paint the picture you need from the scraps that you have. I'll be here for you. Always. You're twenty-four storeys high, suddenly scared.

I'm nineteen now.

Good luck.

I'm on my way down.

Let's do this.

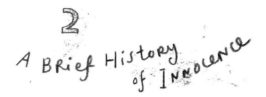

2

A Brief History of Innocence

I was an accident. Born the only son of an academic and an artist on the dot of 1981. Apparently, I was a red and fleshy dead-weight of a baby that learnt quickly and never cried. I don't remember that. We lived in a small village a few bent miles from the coast of Cornwall, our crooked stone cottage alive with quirk and personality, ripe for exploration. Channels of unkempt fern and bramble hedges linked a minute community of retired farmers or elderly, childless couples looking to see out their days in the quiet hum of rural escape. The only other family with kids lived on the main farm in the middle. It perched like a healthy heart, the roads like arteries bringing life in and out with each working day. My earliest memories are of toddling around in muddy lanes, listening for the sound of plastic pipe smacking the last hide of the morning herd, the distant growl of machinery, owls and bats in the evening through mists of midges. I heard the world in rhythms and drones on melodious landscapes, woke up to a world free to roam in, confidently coasting through single digits. Visions of hitting the winner or saving the damsel came vividly in brushstrokes of endless role-play, paradise to conquer in every direction.

This is all very nice, but I notice you haven't mentioned anything about shitting yourself on a regular basis. Too engrossed in your daydreams to want to break character and drop the kids off at the pool? Who knows man, but you did it a lot. Remember that night you were too scared to go downstairs in the dark? You did what anyone would do, of course, and shat in a box of Lego. Poor Mum found the shit bricks and called you a dirty urchin, which is what you were. And how about that time with the school doctor? Down to your kecks please. Walk to the other side of the room please. Bet he regretted that. Bet he was retching as you waddled off, hot cigar swinging from your grundies. Ah, your first encounters with shame. I thought you weren't going to skip bits? It's okay. You got over it. Just get real.

My parents must've tried to love each other once, but communication got sidelined in response to the epiphany that they were entwined, unhappy, but living in a world that meant you had to stay in the race even if you knew you were going the wrong way. Still, they took me where I needed to go and hid their rifts, didn't blame me for their unhappiness.

My bright and busy father was bashfully tall and long-distance thin, always withdrawn, always up against some kind of deadline. Still I worshipped him. I found a way in when I took a kind ear to his record collection—all old stuff. It animated him like nothing else could. He gave me the histories of the greats, swinging his lanky legs, smoking endless cigarettes and sipping from a can of beer, completely obsessed with Bob Dylan. My childhood was carved to a soundtrack of rock 'n' roll wisdom, enthusiastic commentary from Dad, awakened in the eyes of an adoring disciple, preaching to ears ready to accept the sermon. Music was our only dialogue, so I devoured it while I could.

The music, the cigarettes—what a hero. He was everything those album sleeves evoked. He had Pete Townshend's nose and Dylan's dark curls circa New Morning. You ever think about your dad's dad? Your grandpa? Not such a hero. A seldom seen cartoon villain you knew about through whispers. You only met him a handful of times. He was square, but not in an intellectual sense. I mean he was angular—a cubic flattop and a square neck nesting on square shoulders, casting a dark square shadow. I suppose if you're dwelling on your own dad, you should think about his too. Might help you be a little more forgiving. Your dad had to love that oddity! All despite the mythical iron fist, the militant expectations. With not much to go on, you can be sure Grandpa was a bully at best. He forced your old man through the doctorates and degrees, the endless hours of stress and deadlines. Being a biochemist might give you the salary but fucking hell, it doesn't give you a social cushion, just a distinct lack of interaction with people rather than books. If you want to point the finger at anyone for Dad's absence, get it wagging at Grandpa. He was the architect. Think about that for a second before you judge. Your dad's drinking? The chain smoking? That was courage for a deservedly steady hand.

My mum had dark copper hair and blissful green eyes. She was eight years younger than Dad and came from a large family of doctors. The youngest of five, she rebelled against the conformity that surrounded her, broke with tradition and tried to travel and become anything other than what was expected. Somewhere too soon into an ill-planned adventure, she met Dad randomly in the foyer of the Theatre Carré in Amsterdam. He'd noticed her roll her eyes as some geek at the merch desk started throwing his intellect around regarding Leonard Cohen's poetry—her name being Suzanne and all. She saw Dad grinning, and played to it, exaggerating her interest in the bachelor with a sarcastic finger to the chin whenever his eyes averted. Dad, the onlooking stranger, was captivated by her performance—far more entertaining than the musical he'd been enduring. Then she yawned, daring to take the charades further, but the geek caught her. Dad was supposedly in stitches as she blushed red-handed and the young man huffed and walked away, denied. There on a conference, Dad bought her a drink to thank her for the laughs, jesting that the dismissed hopeful actually had some good points about Cohen's prose.

Nine months later, they had me to the sound of three generations saying 'I told you so'. Instead of paying heed to the pleas, they got married and moved south to Cornwall. There, away from the frowns, they could build a home from ideals they figured would fall into place once they had their own space. Dad's genius walked him into a consultancy job at a lab and Mum turned her creativity outdoors, babe on her back as she planted heather and built rockeries, singing musicals in soft soprano. In my mind she's singing opera, but it was probably Cats.

> *Fill in the blanks with romance if you must, but your mum was no Joni. What you loved is that she didn't care. I like to imagine her as a kid vaulting from the banisters and cartwheeling through the house while her siblings were studying. Those fiery locks were only the tail end of some other flame within. To catch your mum with her guard down was as joyful as it got, but that was the first thing to go. She was too isolated, had no outlet. Confidence slips quick when you're out of practice. Oh and by the way—I bet it was the geek that got your dad's attention at the bar in Amsterdam, not her. He loved Leonard. She didn't. It was never going to work. They brought out the worst in each other and would rather hide than admit it. If you need evidence, just remember them taking you to deliver Christmas cards around the village. Trying to plug in to the 'community'. It was certainly a lesson in utmost decorum. Smile politely and accept the widow's jam. Chuckle at yet another ex-farmer's two-hundred-year-old joke that took as long to tell. Soon enough the community spirit waned, the delivery team disbanded and you were sent out solo—the task disguised cunningly as a milestone in your development, but really just an excuse to get out of integrating with anyone themselves. But hey, thank god for that, eh?*

On a Christmas card errand, around eight years old, I knocked on her door. She was my age with mud-brown hair and fearless hazel eyes. I knew her from the bus ride to school but hadn't thought of seeking her out to play before. Seems crazy, but I'd been happy enough in my own head, wasn't missing a friend. Joining me on my rounds was her idea. She threw on a coat and asked if she could come, shouted to whoever could hear and bounced into my world. We recited The Goonies and she taught me how to cup my hands and cuckoo. We raced twig fleets down streams and she dared me to grab an electric fence. As my heart jolted, her infectious laugh echoed through the trees and we became inseparable.

Your very own Joan Baez.

Jess had two older brothers, Daniel and Vincent, who were no doubt in line to take over the farm when they reached adulthood and already well into the initiations. They fought constantly like cubs on the savannah, but it always ended with a hug or a handed-back lock of yanked hair, having been raised to override any grievances and make up unconditionally. It was all alien to me—staring like a tourist on safari.

Jess's mum made ice-cream in rainbows of fresh flavours, and we were chief tasters, our tingling tongues encouraged to criticise if the blackberry too tart or the mint not sweet enough. Isaac, the father, was a big burly man, partial to a knitted jumper and calm as a Hindu cow. The baritone in his voice as he called for Jess to come inside gave me goosebumps. I was but an observer with front-row seats.

Jealous and infatuated in equal measure.

Home had already started to become distant. Dysfunction stirred as Dad's steady hand needed more and more medicine. The pedestal began to crack, the halo fading as the demons awakened. It started as quarrels through stone walls, around corners away from pricked young ears, but such considerations couldn't last forever.

Yeah, volatility likes an audience.

I'd be told to go to my room or play out, dialogue fading along with the dignity that couldn't hold eye contact too much any more. I told myself I didn't mind, that I was probably on my way there anyway. If Jess wasn't around or if it was too late, I'd yank my sheets out from my bed and crawl into a haven of creative escape underneath. My record player—a present from my uncle on my tenth birthday—made its way there along with reams of paper nicked from Dad's office and stacks of pens and pencils in a camouflage lunchbox. I'd don the headphones and scribble stories, poems, comic strips—all to the sound of whatever Dad had been smoking to on his days off.

Everyone you knew became a character. Worlds blurred in a spillage from the pierced hull of your busy imagination and filled up the daydreams in which you were king. These were the moments you locked yourself in, took a deep breath and leapt headfirst, too fast. Fathoming how to map that giddy inner monologue was your guardian angel—a cosmic circus mirror

13

unearthing the warped from the straight and narrow, the meaning from the manners. It all had to go somewhere. Those scribbles were chapter one. If you could read them now, you'd see the value in the madness, the wisdom between the lines. It's not time to think about your books yet though, is it? Okay. We'll get to that.

Things really changed when Dad pushed Mum from halfway up the stairs—drunk for sure, but mindless rather than sinister. While thankfully not hurt, it shook us all. He reached down, cradling the neck of his shaking wife like it wasn't him that had done it. Mum told me she was okay and not to cry. It was the last time I bore witness to any kind of contact between them. I didn't know if I should be thankful. That's when Dad started sleeping in his study. They avoided each other altogether. We all did.

It was scary because it showed what had been lost, but you should be thankful. He saw the consequences of his stupidity, took himself out of the equation. Mum bought a dog and worked a nursing home three days a week—it was hardly Nil By Mouth! You all had your own bubbles and come on, the fantasy world within those bloated pages made far more sense than the real one around you. Also—that isn't when they started sleeping separately. Remember the letter?

I used to like Sunday mornings but it was never because of church. Church wasn't frequent enough to take seriously but I couldn't quite put it from my mind. I got the basic message—be nice, don't have sex yet—but I didn't like the intimidation, the do-this-or-else attitude. Plus I hated the music. Songs about lying in green fields with some old guy in sandals didn't cut it for me. I wanted the heartache and the fugitives from Dad's records.

The devil's music.

I don't remember Mum or Dad thinking much of our holy time. It was more a hangover from their parents who, on scarce visits, would insist on the ritual. What I liked about Sunday was that, before church, the house actually felt alive in its disconnect somehow. A seldom routine—Dad would blast music from his office, smoking menthol cigarettes from green and gold boxes.

Bullion.

Mum would transform from baggy-jumpered farm girl to the irreverent highland beauty she'd once been, eyeing a shy reflection, the morning light breaking into Jacob's through sash windows.

At the kitchen table, just before leaving one day, in a pile of Dad's paperwork, Mum found a letter addressed to her. She winced like she'd stepped off a kerb she hadn't seen, swung out from the table, beckoned Dad out with an anxious glance, closed the door. I assumed the ninja, creeping close and pressing my ear to the wood for mumbled, hissing whispers and the first ripples of conflict. The letter was from Grandpa, on Dad's side. She could tell by the writing and wanted to know why on earth he'd written a letter to *her*?

Dad didn't want to engage, angrily switching the focus to church.

Ninja retreat.

He hurried everyone out else we'd be late, told Mum to read it later. Sat in the back of the car, I could see the envelope sticking out from Mum's coat pocket, and couldn't imagine what secrets it concealed—the forbidden fruit up close and personal. Richard Thompson was on the radio singing about Jerusalem. He was good, but he was no Dylan apparently.

Church itself was the normal fare—deep voices and distant stories on cold, hard pews. Any sense of welcome from the quaint exterior vanished once inside under the suffering eyes of a seven-foot Jesus, sculpted from oily mahogany, backlit. Mum's finger stroked the edge of the letter.

A razor for the wrist.

Dad's head stayed down. The cuffs of his once-immaculate shirt were unbuttoned, spilling out from an ill-fitting blazer. I knew he had booze in his pocket. He always did. Any tremble that had greeted the Lord's dawn would be gone by the time the sermon ended. Sipping in the name of the Father, the Son and the Holy Spirit.

Medicine. Those young mothers that turned their noses up at him on arrival would soon be in his sights—idle

*chit-chat in the car park, a quick wit to the burdens
of church and an enviable confidence. Drinking was
like music.*

The drink seemed like a potion worth investigating
for sure, but I couldn't quite wrap my head around the
trade-off—a couple of hours of extroversion for a whole
evening of upset. In the week he drove and worked long
days, so I'm guessing he wasn't drinking then? Maybe
he was. Either way, home was the place to shut down
and hide now, the booze the one to greet him with open
arms upon return. It seemed to have been the friend
that caught him when he fell and believed him when he
faltered. But now it was twisting, becoming the friend
that he couldn't say no to, the friend that wanted him for
himself—selfish, jealous, bitter, with a devilish talent for
deception. A friend that had once given but now only
knew to take. Indeed, a friend no more.

That's dosage.

After church that day, I was wandering the gravestones
looking for names when I saw Mum read the letter, lean-
ing on the car. It was like she deflated, gut punched by
whatever was spitting from the page. Dad's flirting had
earned him a hand on the arm a few cars away, but the
game ended when Mum screamed blue murder at him
to leave.

She screams like she sings.

She drove. The ride back from church was silent, cold and the last we ever made. A step off the kerb towards rock bottom, and the language of hostility had nothing left to say it seemed. The clouds lulling by in the warm summer skies danced to their own song that day. I was elsewhere.

How old are you here? Tail end of eleven? Must be. You hadn't left primary school yet. You don't think much about primary, do you? I'm guessing that's because it was a breeze. The teachers liked you. You had no enemies. You were pretty much free to exist in cloud cuckoo, occasionally descending to stock up on trivia— the arbitrary stuff you were supposed to be whittling life's spoon with. I get it. Uneventful. So you were eleven, were you? Hmm. A southern breeze is blowing.

I awoke frozen, eyes wide. I'd fallen asleep cramped under the bed again, the record still hissing. I used to love dreaming, but of late I'd been having nightmares— cruel apocalyptic visions of worlds collapsing and not being able to help. There was one in particular that always seemed to precede a fever. I'd wake drenched in sweat and a few days in bed would follow every time, my puffy face hangdog and sizzling. It remains a mystery to me. No articulation could illuminate that one.

Go on, have a go.

I'd be stood outside on a dark, empty shadow of a world. All the horizons were like a sickly black belt of nothing that bled up to even emptier, blacker heavens. I could sense something up there and it was coming for me. I'd try to run, but the gravity was so thick it cramped my body and slurred my steps that rolled the rumbling ground beneath my feet, warping any sense of direction and taking me nowhere. I'd crane my gaze skywards as the universe morphed into a blanket of pins and needles, nauseously throbbing, threatening to fall and swallow everything whole. The air was like a wet tongue on a fresh battery. Behind me, everyone I knew was staring as if I knew something they didn't. I'd try to speak but my breath was ash, my swollen tongue too big for my suddenly parched mouth. My silence angered the crowds and they hissed and seethed. My eyes fizzed, barely able to see and my stomach was sick with fear, no hope on the line. And then it would happen.

The heavens of pins and needles would open. Torrential sickness hammering down as my vision disappeared completely. Familiar voices screamed at me to do something—to save the world somehow—but all I could do was hold out my cupped hands and let the flood disintegrate me.

> *Jesus! That wasn't the nightmare that woke you that night though.*

I couldn't recall the details of the nightmare, but it poked an unfamiliar corner of my mind, shook me roughly from my slumber. I slid out from under the bed and rubbed my bleary eyes, let them dilate and pick up familiarity in the darkness. Outside, the owls hooted melancholy in the moonlight. Relieved to be in reality for a change, I went to get water.

My bedroom was at one end of the house. At the opposing end of the landing was Dad's study at the top of the stairs.

Spiralling patio slabs in chimney crimson with a breezeblock banister.

I paused outside the study, my heart the same tempo as a Howlin' Wolf show-stopper. I hadn't been in there for a long time, but I'd never been told not to. Something about it just felt forbidden.

The light was on, but there was no music coming out so I dared a peak. Dad was in there but he must've been asleep. A creaking fortress of books and files lay in ruin, spilling from the desk and stacked across the floor. Empty bottles sprung up like weeds—bookends to the litter of days gone by. Ash-dank bottle caps were stuffed with countless fag butts and careless muddy footprints left a sad breadcrumb trail from nothing to nowhere. His records lay strewn, expendable, sleeveless. The player was spinning but the music had long since ended. The black circle scratched along with short, hoarse, intoxicated breaths—thirty-three-and-a-third wheezes-per-minute.

With his tall frame hunched in the chewed armchair, Dad's long legs invaded the room. His complexion was an artist's palette done in the skin tones of a breakdown—all dark-vein-blues, liver-spot-purples, the bitten fingernails in cigarette-yellow, a general wash of jaundice in its infancy, scarlet lips and spittle vignette. I wondered what Jess's dad looked like when he slept. Sound, earned slumber most likely.

> *I can see why you'd be thinking that. But why were you also thinking about the time Miss Griggs smacked you at school? You remembered the jam-jar glasses, the mole on her top lip, the hefty wooden ruler. Remember you saw Micky Flint and Penny Ringrose up to no good in the quiet room, thought you'd take the law into your own hands? Such a two-shoes. Well, she didn't care. You got something to say? Save it for somebody else. On bare legs too. Sadist. I never understood your guilt. You were clean. See? Always riding around on someone else's truth. Fuck Miss Griggs.*

On Dad's lap was a half-drunk bottle of martini. They were everywhere. I'd heard of martini in a Dylan song. The bad guys were free to drink it and watch the sunrise when Rubin Carter was in jail—no one doubting that he pulled the trigger. Martini didn't have the romance of something like whisky. Whisky always seemed to be for the good man hard done by. I was disappointed in Dad's poison.

> *You told Jess it was whisky. Kind of sweet really.*

On the wall by the window was a photo of Dad and his younger brother, crooked in a gold leaf frame. Uncle Henry had died not long ago, but I'd never been told how, only that it was a shame. Dialogue around the time became seriously secretive. I could decipher nothing of the uncle I'd met once, who'd given me my first record player and then died a year later in confidential circumstances.

Dad went alone to the funeral up North and returned, another layer of sanity skinned. The picture on the wall had them smiling in front of a cathedral somewhere in the North of England where they'd grown up. You remember that other picture of Henry? Drinking from a jug of beer in a log cabin somewhere in Canada? He looked like your dad, only meaner—brooding eyes laden with mystery. He was a big part of your stories. A shape-shifting, shadowy ghost. Wasn't he the character that went on a pilgrimage to Ontario? From the Neil Young song? Found room and board beneath the stars, forever the victim—so they say. It was better that you drew your own interpretations. Henry was another grail you'd never get your hands on. Even more so than the letter from Grandpa.

A glossy pack of menthol cigarettes winked at me from Dad's desk—an extended filter pointing at me like a bottle in a game of truth-or-dare, all eyes on me. Then I looked at Dad and a junction loomed.

One way a road to intervention, the other to a nice deep sandpit to bury your head. I remember. You imagined grabbing him by the scruff of the neck in your Oscar moment, telling him to straighten out, to love his wife and be happy, firing him from a cannon on a guilt trip towards recovery. Then you looked at the cigarette. You heard the growl of Leonard Cohen, saw the stained fingers of Bob Dylan, the swagger of Lou Reed. You saw yourself years from now at a theatre in the capital, grinding the last jubilant chord of an unwritten anthem, a sweating smoked audience enraptured, red lights down and house lights up. You saw yourself in the dressing room—whisky in hand, Jess on your arm, a hustle of strangers climbing over each other for a moment in your presence, faces from the schoolyard and a man in a blue raincoat offering an invitation to where the real party was. Then menthol lips. You looked good the first time you kissed.

I lit the cigarette and filled my lungs to capacity—hot smoke and secrets. I exhaled as pins and needles rushed through me, bursting the dam of expectations, drowning the initial nausea.

Another deep drag and you had to put it down—a concentrated brew of fairground sickness and cosmic relief.

Polluted.

You collapsed to the floor.

The world as my merry-go-round.

At the foot of your sleeping father, you made your choice.

I Ain't Looking to Compete with You

3

The broken blood vessels around my eye stained the tissue into a squashed plum and there was no hiding it. On the bus home from after-school football, I pressed my forehead against the window, discouraging nosy inclinations from other commuters. I'd never had a black eye before. Never even had a fight. My adrenaline levels were rising again. They'd maxed out in the midst of the scrap. Now they simmered as the anxiety of having to find explanation to Mum took hold. After-school football had been an easy excuse not to go home, but not any more. I needed out—frosty alternative or not.

Scrap is the right word too. What a shambles! Not a sliver of skill between you. Like the blind making hay. But go back a second. Think about how you got there.

Secondary school came with the leap from Tonka Toy minibus to diesel-chugging double-decker and a swathe of new characters to colour my daydreams. On the minibus in primary—once her older brothers had vacated the back seats—the thrones had belonged to Jess and me. We oversaw our kingdom with grace. Seniors' juggernaut was much more of a grizzly dictatorship, clearly defined by seat, age and ego.

We were never going to venture up the back, but that was fine by us, they could have the crowns. We sat out of the way up front, watched as the familiar blur of nettle green and foxglove pink transcended into concrete greys and house-brick reds.

She could've sat anywhere and would've done if not for you.

I was in all the highest classes, but my efforts were directed at keeping the teachers happy and off my back, as opposed to wanting to succeed in the subject.

Teachers are always trying to convince themselves there's worth in their vocation. A talent like you gives them hope. You were capable, and they knew it. Even the ones you didn't get on with. They must've known something of your life outside. There was a general coating of leeway around any of your attempts at defiance, which, let's be honest, weren't exactly criminal. Rebel and conqueror aren't the same thing. You remember that poster competition? It was for the council's revamped roadworks initiative or some shit. They wanted bright, positive vibes, cinematic highways and bold signage. You thought it'd be funny to draw a cartoon of a roadworker holding a stop-go sign with a beer and a fag on. I did like the attention to detail— the oily hi-vis, the bored, bearded face of the guy sat on his arse, one finger gripping the sign in his gold sovereign hand. Mr Salmon didn't get angry, just said you weren't allowed to enter it. He politely called it silly, and wrinkled his avocado-nose. You slipped it into the envelope anyway, and off it went to the council. They laughed so much they came into school and awarded you a £10 book token in front of assembly. Everyone had to applaud as they brought you up to collect it. Old Man Salmon should've eaten his fedora! Big win for you there, man. You'll do well to remember that feeling. That's a lesson in trusting your instincts you won't get in any curriculum.

I liked English. Mrs Griffiths reminded me of Bob from Blackadder. In my first term with her, I wrote a story about a boy that finds a portal under his bed that takes him back to when his parents were kids. I'd bashed it out ten minutes before class. She loved it. She read it out bubbling with pride, directing everyone's attention to the bits they should aspire to.

The next story I wrote, I tried too hard. I overthought the shit out of it in desperation to impress her, make her think I was wise beyond my years. It was about a scientist that got lost in the woods on Christmas day. He found an old church and knocked, but the vicar wouldn't let him in because he didn't believe in god. He froze to death in the graveyard, then came back as a ghost to haunt the vicar, manipulated him into killing his congregation one by one. The last scene was the scientist ghost crossing out the name of the church to read 'Methadone' instead of 'Methodist'. It was fucking awful.

It was fucking genius!

I could feel her disappointment when she handed it back. The grammar was all good—plenty of ticks—but the sparkle in her eye was gone, the head of the nail untouched by a country mile. After that I treated class with bargepole enthusiasm, did just enough to keep coasting.

I dived heavily into my own books, where there was no judgement, and created without interruption. I'd started making album sleeves for made-up bands, coming up with all the track names and imagining the music. I liked making sleeves for The Caution Horses and Cal Hoon. Cal Hoon was a mysterious lady's man puffing black and blue smoke in a blood-red bar. The Caution Horses were a leather-clad rock band à la Guns N' Roses, brought to life in glossy felt tip, with sweating chests and lemon lasers from horned guitars. Guns N' Roses had slipped Dad's 'legends only' net at home a little while back because they did a cover of Knockin' on Heaven's Door, which came bellowing out of his office one day. It was so different to the version I'd known. I didn't even know there was such thing as a cover version. My brain lit up. What was stopping *me* from playing other people's songs? Matter of fact, what was stopping me from writing my own? The song was the king after all. The song was the invention of the wheel, the cover version was just a tyre. I wanted to invent, not manufacture.

That nearly works.

I remembered seeing a guitar gathering damp in the garage at home, shielded by forgotten golf clubs.

It must've been Dad's but I'd never seen him play it. I figured I could rescue and rehouse it.

> *You never liked that garage. It always scared you. It sat unloved across the drive with the tombstone blues.*

I sprinted in and out like Indiana Jones, treasure under my arm.

I didn't know where to begin at first. I studied the guitar on my knees or thwacked the strings in front of the mirror—a proud disturber of the peace imagining what kind of guitarist he'd be once the instrument had been conquered. In senior school I took a few lessons to learn a few songs, get some chords in my fingers. Then I quit.

> *Piece of piss.*

I had enough to breathe life into my songbooks. The floodgates opened.

> *I bet that hurts. Having to admit that it was Guns N' fucking Roses that got you started writing songs? Still, there it is. G, D, C and you were off. By far the most satisfying of your outputs. The heroin of creative endeavours. Be grateful.*

My infancy in the elements meant I was naturally stocky and solid. I was put in all the sports teams because of my rare left foot. Sport came with kudos and was a good way to avoid corridor hostility. Plus Mr Barber, head of PE, was not a man to cross. Old-fashioned and bitter in his methods, he had a short fuse for anyone unwilling to get stuck in—mostly so he could show you how it was done and flatten you into the mud. And woe betide anyone that forgot their kit. You'd be out in your pants doing press-ups over cow shit. Being a part of the team kept his wrath at bay, and trips to other schools for matches were a chance to encounter foreign landscapes and observe new characters.

Let's get this in perspective. In primary school, sure, you were good—a natural even. A little into Year 7 and you were the fastest, highest jumping, longest throwing chubby little fucker out there. However, runner-up every time was Charlie Knowles, unable to even run in a straight line—probably because of the webbed feet. It's not your fault, but you were only King Fish in a tiny puddle. Fast-forward to senior years and the puddle became an ocean, the competition a chump frenzy. It was shocking to discover that you weren't the best at something and even worse to be making enemies because of competence. Throw into the mix the onset and randomness of puberty rearing its cruel head and it's no wonder your reign subsided. How could you be king of a world where just having bum fluff raised your status? You were a slow developer—poor lamb. Remember you nicked your mum's mascara and coloured in the little hairs on your legs to see what adulthood had to offer? Ha ha! Your legs are still ginger, you dope! As well as that, you were no longer a force to be reckoned with on the field. Oppo-

*nents you'd zipped past or caught up to so easily just
a year before were suddenly not taking any shit, going
for your shins, aiming for the windpipe. And the conse-
quence of winning against mono-browed tanks was
very different to how it had been when everyone was
roughly the same size and essentially harmless. Be
grateful you didn't get more black eyes! You could feel
the murky nimbostratus of adolescence looming, just
like the sky in your nightmares. Everything had an edge.
Everything seemed like it might burst like an angry
back boil if you got too close.*

Bravado was a survival kit, crude vernacular, the flint and
steel. If you were lucky enough to have older generations
handing you down slang, you could be a few steps ahead
when the older boys came and sussed you out. They'd
hold their fingers to each other's noses as some kind of
evidence they'd had them down a girl's pants. Claims
of nudity, cum and periods, soggy biscuits, boners and
gashes—it all determined the power structure. And it
seemed if you hadn't masturbated at least twice before
break, you were likely to get your bag emptied out of a
window. I kept my head down or just lied rather than
have to admit to my frigidity.

*You started dreaming about the mysterious vagina
around then. Maybe that was what was falling from
the sky in your fever dreams? An implausible, pulsing
terror coming to swallow you whole? Sounds about
right. That's that mystery solved! Anyway. The new
lingo was a lot of hot air but it was exciting to listen to,*

eh? The imagery it threw up, undoubtedly intriguing.
True, you thought more of the girls being smeared than
the bullshitting boys, but you only ever thought about
calling them out. You never did it. You remained silent
on the subject, your desire for a life without conflict
being crowned top trump. That was until you heard
Jess's name of course.

Chris Llewelyn was a cocky weasel.

Get you!

He was the kind of kid that would see throwing his mates
under a bus as smart. Like me, he hadn't matured physically much, but he kept his rung in the pecking order
by being vindictive, sucking up to the top dogs. I saw
through it early on and tried to steer clear, didn't laugh at
his jokes or give him too much of my time. In the changing room before football practice one day he was holding court to the gullible—his voice up and down in pitch
like a cartoon teen. He claimed he'd lost his virginity to
a Year 10 after sharing a bottle of 20/20 and 'flicking her
chin'. I guess he meant for it to sound like a cool, romantic gesture, but the way he said it just sounded funny to
me. The thought of him flicking a girl in the face with his
yoghurty finger made me laugh out loud. I was lacing my
boots when a glob of phlegm hit my forehead and slid
down my eyebrows, ill and green.

'What's funny, Ginge?' Chris, licking his lips, shoulder
to shoulder with his audience.

I wiped my head with my sleeve, irritated but not enough to retaliate. I moved along the bench rather than stoke the fire. Mr Barber would be in soon, curtly hushing everyone away, but Chris continued with the bullshit. I tried to zone it out, but he was aiming my way now, prodding and teasing. And then somewhere in the mud—'Jess'.

I didn't hear what was around it. Neither did I need to.

'Fucking hell you're dumb, Chris.'

'Yeah?' He lit up—the baiting successful. 'Just coz you want to finger Jess but she hasn't got a dick.'

I looked up from my boots, 'How does that work then?'

'Erm coz you're gay, maybe?'

I couldn't wrap my head around that one.

'So hang on, I'm gay but I want to finger a girl and I'm what? Angry? Upset? That the person I want to finger *hasn't* got a dick? I sound very conflicted, Chris!'

He glazed over.

'Yeah? Ginger spastic!' he spat dumbly.

'You're not allowed to say spastic, Chris. *Remedial* is the word you're looking for. Ginger remedial. Isn't that what it says on your bag? So you don't get lost?'

> *CRACK!! That was the black eye. So cheap he should've been paying you. You were sat down for fuck's sake! I know he wasn't there for the literary jousting, but Jesus. You'd never been punched in the face before and you'd never seen it happen like that either—such clean contact, just like a movie. You'd seen fists flying and red-faced, dinner-line scuffles, but you'd also seen how those things got mythologised and exaggerated. Things you'd discern*

*as arbitrary swinging became tales of skilful execution
and gossip about fighting styles with post-match analysis and a fictional leader board.*

I locked eyes with Chris, standing with a puff of the chest.
He lunged again but I saw it this time, instinctively grabbing his arms and thrusting us into fraught nonsense—
much more like the skirmishes I'd seen. It was all pretty
blurry but I definitely had him in a headlock at some
point, surprised and excited at the discovery that if this
was a fight I think I was winning.

*He underestimated you and was suffering for it. All
those years of hay bale dens and rope swings—you had
him! You should've fish-hooked his eyes and kneed the
ventricles from his nose, stomping your studs into his
veg like John Barnes prepping the penalty spot. Instead
you elbowed him like an old lady puffing up a cushion and pulled his shirt over his face. What was that?*
Women In Love?

I took a slew of body hits but I hung on to him, squeez-
ing, hoping the storm would pass. The audience was
eerily silent. There were no sides. I think everyone
was just shocked that I was on top. I let go of him and
he staggered back flustered and embarrassed. My lip
was bleeding and I had the stain of broken veins starting to warm around my eye. Chris had slimed his way
out of looking like he'd been in a fight at all. Despite
this, he knew and everyone else in that changing room
knew that I could've had him no question if I'd wanted.

34

Chris didn't want to take that risk. Lucky for him Mr Barber came striding in with his clipboard of last names. Everyone scarpered like kitchen-lit cockroaches back to their pegs, silent witnesses.

Mr Barber ushered everyone out to the playing fields, thankfully unaware of the last few minutes, and training continued uneventfully. There were no signs of retribution. Chris even tried to pally up to me on the pitch, but I didn't want to be friends. His reputation had taken a beating and mine had been given an unwanted boost, the other kids seeking to congratulate me having now picked their side. I didn't like it. I could see the days ahead—the facts seeding the myths, the new view of me as someone to be reckoned with, the inevitable challengers threatened by fresh meat on the block. I got changed and ran to the bus stop.

> *And we're back there again, homeward bound with the events blurring in your mind like the fields through the windows. Your eye was now an obvious war wound though you hadn't actually seen it yet. You knew it was bad because Mr Barber had taken you aside after practice, said no words, but looked at your face like a right old fiend, a dirty purple smirk in his bloodshot cheeks. Like whatever had happened was no more than a life lesson he'd give the students himself if the powers would only allow.*

I was two minutes from home but hadn't visualised a satisfactory scenario with Mum to warrant going there just yet. I hadn't got my story down. I'd see if I could find Jess, buy some time.

She was outside her house filling dog bowls from a bucket. I stood behind the sycamore at the end of her drive, called her over. Adolescence hadn't changed her much—still warm and thoughtful, petite and athletic, her dishevelled tomboy hair tucked loose behind her ears. Stability kept her character in check. She got plenty of attention from boys at school but it hadn't occurred to her to investigate. She was too unimpressed having grown up around two boisterous older brothers—she'd seen it all before.

I told her about the fight. I recounted my defence of her good name and found myself laughing at the slapstick of it all, the retelling sending a surge of testosterone through my giddy body. She was upset but laughed too, couldn't wait to get her hands on Chris the weasel and give him a good kicking herself. I didn't tell her about my fears of retribution—my theory remaining that Chinese whispers would be making for a bumpy road ahead in the corridors. She always brought out the reasonable in me, stifled the overthinker.

She leant in and hugged me, which wasn't in itself unusual—we'd grown up as tactile friends—but something about it this time felt different. More solid, less comprehensible.

She let go and you wanted her to do it again, but she'd run off to get a jumper. She was coming back so you could walk to the river-swing and talk some more. But you'd changed your mind, said you had to go home. You

said you could probably sneak past Mum and even if
she did catch you, you'd decided on the sooner-rather-
than-later philosophy. Jess understood.

She hugged me again. It was briefer than the last, but still a healthy dose of intangible. I sprinted home through the lanes, dead centre. A tan car with a mustard door lit me up in its headlights, honking sharply as it dodged by. Mum was in the back garden puffing a cigarette. I went straight in through the front door, holding my breath as I bounded silently up to my room, collapsing on the bed as I emptied my lungs. My damaged eye was out of sight, out of mind. I climbed under the covers and masturbated into my boxers, taking off and landing within seconds.

A cocktail of guilt, regret and ecstasy. And just like the
legend of the cigarette, it was the first, but of course it
wouldn't be the last.

4 Let Me Clip Your Dirty Wings

Dad had been written off sick from work. I only knew because he was always home. We didn't speak. He cut an ever-slimming shadow dressed in whale-grey pyjama bottoms and a Hot Tuna t-shirt that looked like it was trying to swallow him whole. I saw glimpses of a ghost searching for meaning in forgotten walls.

He tried to busy himself with DIY. Days would begin soberly gathering tools, but nothing ever got finished. I'd leave for school and come back to a different home—domestically vandalised—and dad drunk in his office listening to Dylan. Stripped doorways and half-painted walls, planks of wood like pick-up-sticks, sawdust piles and the stench of turpentine, with stiffening rags and brushes everywhere. Dad's Stanley blade had sliced up the kitchen lino, leaving thoughtless stepping stones of old brown glue. The house decayed with the home. It was a cry for help, but who knew? Mum came from a long line of head buriers, and Dad's soberest moments were convincing enough for her not to have to incite drama, I guess. I found solace in my head. We were all ships in the night.

Mum had bought another dog. That was three now. Three dopy spaniels—Dodger, Oliver and Fagin. They took up her time, gave her the distraction she deserved and the companionship she needed. I joined her on walks sometimes where she talked to the dogs a lot. Our own conversations were only skin deep—the weather, sometimes school. It wasn't so much not knowing what to say, as not knowing how to say it. We exchanged headlines but never ventured into details. I told her I'd started a band and joined the school play, which she seemed to like. She said, 'Practice makes perfect.'

> *Ah yes, joining the school play. Well spotted. My hat's off to you, good sir, that was quite the stroke of genius. Mr Barber just laughed when you quit the football team. He reddened and rolled his piss-hole eyes, judging you to be the queer he'd always suspected. Fucking paedo. But what could he do? Rehearsals for the play were the same night as football and GO FUCK YOURSELF, FLOYD!!*

I was in the chorus for Jesus Christ Superstar. It was safe and easy. Drama introduced me to a world I'd never seen—like-minded dreamers and misfits full of fantasy.

> *Better than that, it introduced you to grunge. Thank you, Simon. Yes, he is pleased to see you.*

Simon played Judas with a blistering tenor from surfers' lungs. He was a couple of years older with confidence and charisma to die for. He took his gold-top Gibson and bottle of ginger beer everywhere he went, Marlborough Lights in one pocket, Walkman in the other. He painted his fingernails black but didn't need eyeliner, his eyes already defined beyond his years.

He taught me everything he knew about grunge—Meat Puppet riffs, Thurston's feedback, Cornell's soul—but most of all, everything he knew about the newly fallen prince of it all, and my new hero, Kurt Cobain.

Grunge had the ingredients I never knew I needed. It was medicine. A miracle cure for being a misfit. Dad's records were harder to get hold of these days, but I'd never thought of anything bettering the classics, hadn't looked beyond what I already knew. How wrong I was. Guns N' Roses hadn't quite clinched it.

Sure they hadn't.

This was something else entirely. I'd fallen asleep on the edge of a cliff and woken to find I was falling, springing desperately to life and in need of a solution. In grunge I'd found one, in the most blissful of philosophies—fuck it! And vinyl was out, tapes were in. No more time-consuming rituals, I could main line. Mum bought me a CD/tape combo and I ripped out the brambles up the side of the house to keep myself in albums.

Nothing like a fresh obsession.

Simon took me under his wing.

He liked you. He took a shine when he showed you how to play Back in Black and you blew him away with how quickly you nailed it. He nicknamed you Angus.

I can see how you'd misread the signs. He was pedestal bound at first sight and worthy of a jerk or two, right?

We started a band called Oblivion. I designed a logo and made a clock of it in woodwork. Simon wrote the songs. They were really good.

Bollocks. I draw the line on this one. Take your head out of your arse. He was a flaccid Billy Corgan copycat at best. You can't sing about heartache if you've been so lucky as to have straight teeth and a silver spoon up your arse. It was bullshit—didn't work. What? You love him or something? Your songs were way better. At least they meant something. But then look what happened. Just like with Miss Griffiths in English, you tried too hard to impress and lost your touch. Don't be down on yourself. His ego wouldn't have let him be seen singing the lyrics of a Year 9 anyway, no matter how good the song was. But that wasn't why you were in the band. You know that. Why you being a dick?

He knew I was friends with the untouchable Jess. I should've known, but I was too caught up in his perfume, blinded by need.

Desire.

I was disappointed that we only rehearsed once a week, but I was still keen to show the world at the talent competition at the end of term. Simon was flaky, made excuses. I ended up in the show on my own screaming Pennyroyal Tea to a bewildered gaggle of bored parents. Not my own. Simon didn't enter the competition at all. He said it wasn't the real deal if your audience hadn't paid to come and see you.

Rehearsals dropped off but he was still always looking for me around school, keen to hang out despite the age difference. We made mixtapes for each other and he was always asking about where I lived. He said he used go to the ice-cream parlour when he was a kid, said he'd love to see it again sometime. He asked if he could come to the village bonfire night. I couldn't have been quicker to say yes.

> *Ah, bless. You thought it would be an evening birthing anecdotes—chapter one of rock history's greatest duo. That was a good mixtape you made him. A little Mudhoney heavy, but cool cover. You had a thing about dummies hanging from nooses. You put the secret track from Nevermind at the start, knowing he hadn't heard it. Some fan! What a fake. Kurt Cobain had not long killed himself. He did it with a shotgun—pulled the trigger with his toes. They printed his suicide note in the NME and you wanted it tattooed on your chest or on the pit of your 'burning, nauseous, stomach.'*

When Simon arrived he gave me a bear hug and a copy of the Singles soundtrack, couldn't have been happier to see me. And then Jess arrived and the gears shifted. I became the expendable little brother at the butt of his wit, there to inflate his ego. Jess couldn't take her eyes off him, giggling in his aura as he cast me aside to pursue his bounty. He unlocked something in her I hadn't seen before. I remember staring at the fire, knowing they were behind me, closer than necessary.

There's no way she was cold. Not with that sheepskin. Not that close to the fire. Love's first flicker like a burning effigy.

I was secretly scheming a dramatic solution. I wanted to spin around and grab Jess, kiss her astonished lips, stun the pair of them into silence and not get any attention from the adults. Then I'd whisper sweet justifications to her and she'd follow me home, leaving Simon like the limping kid in the Pied Piper. We'd go to my room, talk, kiss some more, then...

I shook off the fantasy as lust loomed.

Sweet justifications? What were you going to say? You know I think I'd rather recall another story about you shitting yourself than dwell on whatever sickly drivel you were contemplating. Funny isn't it? How someone that has a way with words can produce such utter tosh? Yin and Yang I suppose. Getting to know the spectrum. Well, thank god you didn't get to do it. You were waiting for your eyes to water—to really give the scene some power—but you left it too late, you melon.

'What you doing, Angus?'

It was Simon. How long had I been staring at the flames? Despite the heat, I froze. Panic en masse from every direction, running reds and headed for the junction where reality met the fantasy I'd dived a little too deep into. Code Red on the nuanced theatre, I'd have to switch up and do something drastic.

Before I knew it, I'd grabbed a log from around the pyre and hulked it violently into the heart of the heat. Embers shot outwards in a swarm of boiling fireflies. Adults gasped and farm dogs jumped to attention—all eyes on me, rigid as November steel. Guy Fawkes rolled off in a smoking heap. A beat of disbelief went by and, with the sense that a responsible adult was about to reprimand me, I turned to Jess, my worries about causing spectacle vanishing.

'Happy, Jess? Let me know what it feels like won't you?'

I kicked at another log but basically just stubbed my toes like an idiot. More gasps and Jess's dad in silhouette striding towards me.

'Fuck it!' I yelled, bolting from the scene. I didn't see Jess's face and she said nothing.

You should've thrown Simon onto the pyre. Singed his Judas locks.

When I made it home, the house was lifeless apart from the telly where Mum sat and the usual frosty light oozing down the stairwell from Dad's office. The concrete banister had Dad-sized handprints in dripping crimson going all the way up. It caught my eye but was too much reality to comprehend at that time. Whatever the hell Dad was thinking when he did that was of no concern to me at that moment. I slammed the flaking door and Mum nearly jumped out of her skin. I darted up past the latest decorating disaster, following dark red drips that led to Dad's study. I glanced left briefly to catch the sight of a sleeping Dad, but my focus was getting to my room as dramatically as possible. Mum was behind me at the foot of the stairs, now in quick pursuit. I shut myself in my bedroom and pulled a chair in front of the door as Mum knocked.

'What's wrong?' she said. 'This isn't like you.'

How the fuck did she know?

She said I shouldn't keep things from her.

Laughable!

I yanked the door open and my swivel chair somersaulted across the room as Mum stared at her son the stranger. I had so much I wanted to say but as usual could only manage a headline.

'What don't you understand, you moron?'

You remember what I said about tosh?

I shut the door in her face and jumped onto the bed, silent but for heavy breathing and Mum's defeated footsteps across the landing. I rolled onto my front and let my hand swing down like smashed champagne. I'd outgrown my den underneath. It was dream storage now.

Didn't stop you though. You slid to the floor and under, pushing the boxes of songs aside. Your record player was still there, Dylan's Oh Mercy still gathering dust from who knows when? You pushed the button and the carousel awoke. You lay on your back and reached into your pocket, lighting another stolen cigarette. They were easy pickings these days. Dotted around and going to waste if you didn't smoke them. The ladle in your mind soup slowed to a crawl, reality fading with each menthol blast, as you drifted away to the sound of Dylan's prophecies.

Most of the time, I'm clear focused all around. Most of the time.

I'll take it from here. Needs to be said. Needs to be undiluted. You were truant for the first time, staring out your bedroom window. Mum had taken the dogs out, which meant you'd risen from your pit disobediently. Kurt Cobain was on your mind. You wished he was still alive. You'd been playing Heart-Shaped Box, but worried you were being too loud. You didn't want to get Dad's attention. He was home somewhere, racking up the failures. You heard footsteps on the gravel outside and had to duck down when you saw Dad tripping across the driveway towards the garage. As you peeked from the sill, he moved with purpose, a long length of hose coiled over his shoulder. He freed the doors with a heavy-handed yank and exposed the empty cave to a smattering of daylight. You watched carefully as he turned and headed for the car. He threw the hose onto

the passenger seat and followed into the driver's, turn-
ing over the cold engine—violent revs from leaden feet,
pistons piercing the autumn.

I remembered being six or seven when Dad ribbed me
for staring at Jess as she cycled by one morning. I cried
and threw my bowl of raspberries at him. As a way of
apologising he built a games field in the back garden—
fence-post wrestling ring, snapped branch goalposts
with washed-up trawler net, bowed stick and bailer
twine archery set, apple skittles, and washing-line high
jump. I squeezed him tight and couldn't wait to let the
games begin. Then I had to swallow as he turned for the
house, an engagement from the adult world beckoning
and me left to do battle with myself and my imagination
once again.

Out with the trash and the fairies. You were also dwell-
ing on last night's antics at the bonfire, enjoying the
possibility that you'd wedged some distance between
Jess and Judas, buzzing at the public embracing of your
new 'fuck-it' philosophy. The school bus would've been
agony but lucky for you the skiving swindle was a piece
a cake—Mum knocked, you ignored! Anyway. Where
were we? Mustn't get sidetracked now. Your dad revved
the engine and stuck the car in reverse, forgetting to
shut the door. He shot towards the empty garage with
the subtlety of a nail bomb, holding course as the car
door wrenched back like a piece of Lego. Remember the
grind of the handbrake teeth, the engine still running,

the warm revs choking in a dead end of breezeblocks? He tumbled out of the car and dragged the jettisoned door out of the way. He didn't seem bothered by it. It didn't seem to matter at all. He climbed back in and continued reversing, the brake lights colouring the dark a murderous red as he stopped. You looked on, shaking your head, no pedestal able to withstand the avalanche of indifference. He climbed out again and squeezed down the side of the damaged car, tugging at the garage doors, wedging the swollen wood shut with him inside. Remember the rusted drop bolt punctuating the scene with paradiddles as he shook the doors violently into their final resting place? And nothing but a raised eyebrow from you. You were thinking about skiving off school again tomorrow. And with Dad out of the house at least you could play a song. But not Nirvana. You couldn't sing that quietly so you turned to old faithful—the first you ever learnt.

Mama, take this badge from me.

Lungs gasping, you yawned wide. You hadn't been sleeping much. One last look at reality and you were bed ways, your body succumbing to shutdown. You could hear the muffled engine. You could hear diminished thrush choirs committed to autumn song from glossy wet branches. You could hear Dodger, Oliver and Fagin yapping up the lane—echoes bouncing around stripped November trees. Mum was on her way home. You'd be elsewhere by then. Eyes closing, you dived head first into a dark melodious ocean. Deep last breaths adrift weightless beneath the howling waves of a reality too confusing to bear, too bewildering to embrace.

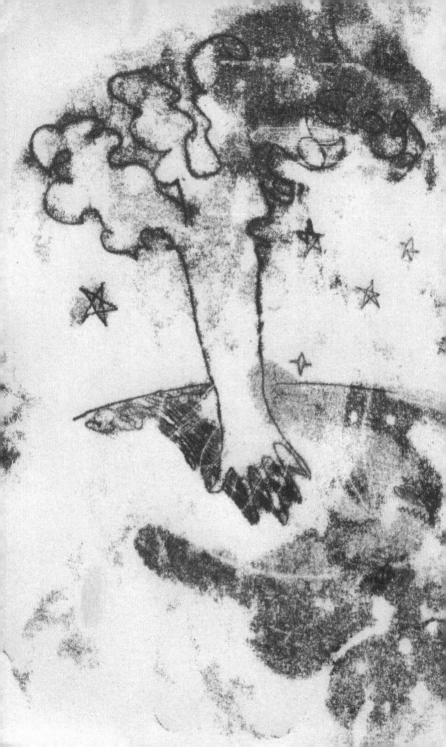

5 To Dust,
I Guess,
Forgotten And Absorbed

Wake up.

At the foot of the Manawatu gorge on the North Island of New Zealand, a dirt track disappears into cavernous swathes of nikau palms and podocarp trees. Like a dry reptilian tongue, it coils out from dark green jaws, spreading as it fades into a thirsty fork, the hot ground plateauing into one of many hundreds of acres of farmland. As the white sun dropped from cloudless skies, I was sat in the back of a pickup truck, speeding from inside the belly, headed out from the shade into the open air. I had a twenty-gauge rifle across my lap, wearing a Sonic Youth t-shirt and typically knee-less jeans. My shoulder-length, sun-rust hair moshing freely. It was New Year's Eve, 1996.

Sonically, I could make out tuis and kāhus at the high end, the shifting of palms in the wind like a wire brush on a loose snare. The rattle and hum of the axle beneath provided a bassy, rumbling music bed. Somewhere in the mid-frequency was a symphony of insects, but their voices were soft, couldn't cut through the noise of the truck. I was imagining the ground thick with beetles and wetas, cicadas and spiders scurrying in a blanket so thick you couldn't stop the truck for fear of infestation.

I smiled at the thought of breaking down, imagining my escape.

In the back with me was my cousin Hamish. He was the son of Mum's oldest sister, Aunt Kath. Unlike me, he'd escaped the highlander genes and had much of the strait-laced Danish heritage from his dad, Uncle Paul's side—rose skin, neat mousey hair, long dark lashes circling two robin's-eggs. A crossbow lay across his juddering legs, held in place by a bandaged hand. I'd always known I had a cousin, but we'd never met until the move.

Mum and I arrived a month or so ago after an empty year waiting for citizenship and thirty hours in transit via Denpasar and Cairns. I struggled to sleep on the plane, so I read Trainspotting and devoured de-cussed Hollywood to pass the time. An emotional Aunt Kath met us at the airport and drove us a final twenty minutes to her home in Norseville—a blink-and-you'll-miss-it town on the other side of Manawatu. I must have finally nodded off in the car, as I don't remember the ride, pulling up the drive or even stepping out of the car and into the house. Bags at our feet in the hallway, I was introduced through crusty eyes to Hamish. He was a year older, smart and with a permanent cheeky grin. Aunt Kath was beginning to blubber again, but quick to assure me all was going to be well by giving both me and Hamish brand new skateboards. Hamish saw our forced friendship as an excuse to get away from sentiment. He asked me if I was fifteen yet in a freshly broken Kiwi accent.

'Nearly sixteen.' I said.

'You wanna drive then?' producing a set of keys from his pocket.

Mum's green eyes cut a sharp glare at her nephew who smirked nervously, realising he'd loosened the knot on a certain bag of cats. Aunt Kath broke the tension by telling us to take our skateboards to the warehouse, her accent a marble cake of opposing hemispheres. Hamish was already out the door. I called after him.

'What warehouse?'

Outside on the driveway, we jumped into a black Land-cruiser. Inside was a mess—a work vehicle for sure. Pink and yellow invoices and order sheets were folded and stuffed in every crevice, two-a-penny company biros and empty shotgun shells scattered the dashboard, oily marks on cream interior gave clues to varying culprits with guilty fingers. There was a petrol can in the footwell and the unvarnished stock of a crossbow on the back seat, a five-disc CD player and automatic gears.

Hamish let me in on the secret Mum had been keeping from me. In New Zealand, you only had to be fifteen to get your driving licence. I couldn't wait. My jet lag hangover was ebbing away, the toll of the long-haul flight purging as I snapped into focus on my new reality, the wild heights of my vivid imagination paling in comparison to the movie set I'd just woken up in.

Thousands of acres of hills and plateaus surrounded a small town that from Hamish's house you could gaze upon in its entirety. The next closest house was a quarter mile away, and then another, and a couple more till the terrain obstructed any sense of community and long roads split into empty tracks leading to either town or wilderness. I turned to look at the house behind as Hamish twisted the keys, the engine purring somewhere down around E flat. The house was magnificent, designed and built by Uncle Paul. Like a proud castle, it sat on its own two or three acres of land, a track worn in around the edges and a wooded patch across the paddock with a wild stream slithering through.

Hamish hit the gas and we sped off the drive down a grit track, my fatigue waking to another level as a Pearl Jam song I hadn't heard before came screaming out of the stereo. At the junction, Hamish yanked the handbrake. Skid marks released a billow of dust as he pulled down hard right, liberating the brake and finding give in the gas, perfect drift, whipping off towards town. I gripped the armrest, suppressing my delirium. He asked me if I wanted to build a ramp, but already knew the answer.

With the windows down, we cruised along Norseville's high street. I think I saw something similar in one of the inflight movies. Something about the locals running strangers out of town in small-time America? Right and off the high street, white wooden houses spread into blocks on roads three times as wide as I'd ever seen. They all had red corrugated roofs and decked verandas, were built on waist-high stilts on lawns separated by pole and chicken-wire fences. There was a Maori family hanging out on one of the porches—from great-greats to infants, barbecue, beers and singing. Some shot the breeze across the fence with neighbours and spun nieces and nephews in the garden—a leg and a wing to see the king. They were beaming and high on life. Muscular, tattooed men, laughing with their eyes closed, walnut buzz cuts and dark tea skin. Women as beautiful as I'd ever seen—coils of lush mahogany hair draping over athletic shoulders, lips full, eyes like chocolate. A teenager jumped from the veranda to the ground.

'Why are the houses on stilts?' I asked.

'Earthquakes.' said Hamish, turning down another studio lot. They'd be nothing but splinters without the stilts, he said. No foundations.

'How come yours isn't on stilts?' I wondered.

Hamish smirked. 'We can afford bricks.'

With my own eyes I'd only ever seen one person with dark skin before. It was at an athletics meeting in Cornwall, back when I was playing the role of teacher's pet and schools from all over the county met up to compete for tacky trophies. I was sat around the three-hundred-metre mark with some other kids—refreshing orange wedges and grassy knees. A pistol went off to my left and indecipherable voices burst from crowds of children like thousand-inch cymbals. Eight kids flew past. One of them was black and he was slaughtering his opponents, yards ahead immediately and the gap growing. A kid to my right, that I'd never bothered getting to know, swivelled to face me. He was eating a yoghurt with his fingers.

'Shall I tell you why black people are so fast?'

I was already wincing.

'Because in India where they come from they have to chase their food.'

I couldn't get angry. Didn't know where to start. A cow's lick sprouted from his shaved snooker-ball bonce and a gold stud in his ear warned me not to antagonise. He was the kind of kid that would've poured salt on slugs and thrown darts at sparrows—his skull completely empty. He used two fingers to get every last glob from every last crease in his fusty peach melba. In my head I offered prayer to Dylan for my worldly education—for singing of Oxford Town where guns and clubs followed you down if your face was brown, of Emmett Till, Rubin Carter and poor Hattie Carroll, slain by a cane twirled around a white, diamond-ring finger. Thank you Bob, forever and ever. Amen.

The warehouse that Aunt Kath had been talking about was the family-run steelworks. Hamish reversed into the courtyard, jumped out and started wisecracking with the workers like he was one of them. We helped ourselves from stacks of steel lasagne sheets, took rods and girders, dodged beeping vans and forklift trucks. We tied every-thing down to a trailer with a ratchet crank, hitched it to the Landcruiser and were off again, back to the house and a massive workshop to get the welder and the angle grinder going. We talked Smashing Pumpkins and an hour later, with very little input from me, Hamish had finished building a quarter pipe from steel like it was nothing. It was pretty mind-blowing to watch. I was just trying to remain socially tuned in, creating a new version of myself just to keep up—a persona that was practical and allowed for lightning spontaneity.

Hamish wheeled out a black hose and a gas canis-ter, asked me if I'd ever used an airbrush. I felt a twinge of nervousness at the thought of painting anything. A memory from infancy fluttered by—making handprints in duck-egg blue across newly stripped walls with Dad, upgrading from cot to single bed and a new chapter in my childhood. I didn't want to think about it.

PFSSSSS!!!! PFSSSSS!!!!

Hamish squeezed the trigger on the hose, spitting bullets of compressed air.

PFSSSSS!!!! PFSSSS!!!!

On the ramp, in silver, I sprayed an alien with bulging black eyes shaking an airplane in its fist, the passengers' faces Munch with horror. In loud pink letters I wrote,

TAKE ME TO YOUR DEALER

We skated around the drive till dark. I'd done a little before and was streets ahead of Hamish technically. What he had was guts. His thing was careering down the drive towards the ramp with nothing in mind other than lift-off. Stacking it didn't seem to faze him, he'd just get up, pick broken tarmac from his elbows and try again.

As the sun disappeared, he reversed the Landcruiser over and lit us up. The stereo kicked in. Pearl Jam again. I knew some of their early stuff but Kurt Cobain had ripped into them in an interview once, said he'd always hated their music. I'd been a good disciple and followed his lead. This though? I loved it.

'Fuck you, Kurt.' I muttered under my breath as Hamish turned it up, another belter I'd never heard.

'What else you got?' I asked.

'Heaps!'

He reached under the seat and pulled out a carry case of CDs the size of a suitcase. Had it not been for my jet-lagged body finally insisting on shutdown, I'd have sworn I was already asleep—dead in fact, and risen in heaven!

You done yet?

Summer in New Zealand meant extended holidays over Christmas and New Year before school started again. I'd just had an English summer. With the timing of the move I was getting two in a row. Mum and I were to stay in the busy family home over the holidays while she looked for a house in town. My Kiwi family were super bright and the house was riddled with signs of achievement. Shelves that creaked with trophies and science books rose from floor to ceiling. An ancient violin hung on the wall beside countless framed certificates and pictures of Uncle Paul shaking hands with various suits. There was an upright piano in the living room—no television—but an all-mediums hi-fi and giant maple speakers.

The workshop outside was full of blacksmith tools, bottles of chemicals, tins of paint and fertiliser. The keys for two quad-bikes hung from an antler. Another set of keys were in a box above the door. They were for the gun rack—two shotguns, a twenty-gauge and a 303. Unbelievably, it was all at our disposal and Hamish was very keen to induct me. I'd been nervous about shooting possums at first, but was told they were a pest and it was necessary. Plus I didn't want to disappoint Hamish. I jumped on the coat-tails of what was the closest thing to a brother I'd ever get and was soon blasting beady eyes from the trees with lip-licking glee.

In the evenings, being present was a staple value of the home. As well as me, Hamish, Aunt Kath, Uncle Paul and Mum, there was my other cousin, Frances—eighteen and home from university. She was very hip and laid-back. Popular with the boys no doubt. She brought friends round to stay and they laughed and listened to Pink Floyd, wore short shorts and bikinis under surf-brand vests. I was welcome in their presence but I was way too self-conscious. I sat on the outskirts mostly, imagining things I might say had I had the guts.

Things you might say and do.

I'd never known I was scared of heights until I climbed the cliff at Drake's Bay. Like a lemming I followed Hamish, but had to bail when I saw the drop. I climbed cautiously back down and skimmed stones red-faced by the water's edge while he back-flipped from the pinnacle, calling me a fag.

Struggling to hold on to the mask now, aren't we?

Making pipe bombs was a far safer pastime. I could get on board with that. Clamp one end in a vice and fill it with gunpowder. Then clamp the other and drill a small hole to poke a fuse in, taping it down to trap the oxygen. Simple. By the time you lit it and got twenty feet away, the glue melted and the fizz got in with splendid results.

After we'd blown up some empty paint cans we spread our destructive wings, used thicker pipe, stronger powder, blew up *full* cans of paint in the woods, the trees splattered in shocks of dripping wet magnolia, mint and citrus. More sophisticated concoctions followed of course, Hamish never one to sit still. A few weeks after we'd met, I ran into the garage at the behest of a cry from him. He was stood over a bucket, slowly stirring around a smaller bowl floating in the middle on iced water. He was making a smoke bomb, had brown jars of salt-petre and bags of fertiliser spilling on the counter. He needed me to keep stirring the bucket while he ran to get ice and salt. He'd overcooked the potassium nitrate apparently and needed to keep the temperature down else it would blow up in his face. No big deal! I nervously asked him how cold we needed to keep it. He laughed and pointed vaguely at the thermometer hanging over the lip of the bucket.

'About there.'

'And where can't it get to?' I asked.

He laughed again, moved his finger an inch or so.

'About there.'

We were going to light the bomb outside the school—one of the few places with streetlights. Our intention was to speed off to the end of King's Road and watch the smoke engulf the streets from a distance. The tip of the fuse wouldn't catch, so Hamish moved in, holding the flame dangerously close to the bomb itself. Suddenly, the potion seized on the heat, hungry for the spark to inject life into its chemical slumber. It fizzed and flared up, scolding Hamish's hand. He yelped and ran to the car, thick blue smoke already pouring out in the amber hue of quiet suburbia and clearly out of our control. Laughter turned to panic as we leapt into the car and sped off, thick fog smothering the evening in triumphant billows of mischief. Curtains on the street pulled back, porches lit up and dogs howled—the peace most definitely disturbed.

Hamish had burnt his hand pretty badly. He'd seared the skin on his palm clean off. He hadn't been able to keep it from Aunt Kath, though he tried for a few hours until the endorphins waned and the pain kicked in. We had no choice but to confess. We got grounded over Christmas for a week, our release date was to be New Year's Eve.

Best thing that could've happened to you.

Mum couldn't bring herself to get angry with me. She knew I was passenger to most of the mischief and just asked that I didn't do it again. She was looking for work and had found a house for us to move into in the New Year. Things were going to be okay.

Christmas was a short affair and didn't come with much fanfare. Three festive days was enough for my straight and serious uncle. To him, indulging in it was a waste of precious work hours. I swore you could hear cogs clanging in his brain—systematic and mundane in their rhythms. He had high expectations for Hamish to follow in his engineering footsteps and every moment counted.

Hamish spent his incarcerated week finishing off the crossbow he'd started lathing in the garage, Uncle Paul watching closely over his shoulder. I could either watch or find my own focus. Luckily, Aunt Kath had bought me an electric guitar for Christmas, which solved that dilemma. My acoustic guitar was in transit from England along with the quarantined dogs and the rest of our stuff. My boxes of songbooks were on their way too, but I didn't want to face them yet or write anything new. Instead, I set about learning everything in the Pearl Jam catalogue, note for note. In a week of confinement I learnt Ten and Vs., couldn't wait to get onto my favourite, Vitalogy. Fuck you, Kurt.

Welcome back! That was some deep hibernation. I need to gather myself again, get focused. And hey, go easy on Kurt. It wasn't his fault.

I hoped my singing would be heard through the walls by Frances and her friends. I imagined them whispering about me, fantasised about getting a knock on the door.

Yeah? What would you have done?

New Year's Eve—the day of release—sat in the back of the pickup truck, speeding away from Manawatu, it was the first time Hamish and I had been out since the smoke bomb. Uncle Paul was driving, having taken us on a failed hunting jaunt. The unsuccessful mission had irked him but it really pissed off Hamish, keen to christen the weapon he'd been slaving over. We were heading home now to prep for the party they were hosting— reluctantly in my uncle's case. Staring at the cinematic landscape could make you think you were dreaming, but the bandage on Hamish's hand was a very real reminder of my situation. He was a time bomb of his own creation. I felt it best if I disconnected.

> Turns out making bombs and killing vermin wasn't as exciting as figuring out the drop D tuning in Even Flow or singing lines like 'her legs spread out before me' in your newly broken voice.

We arrived up the drive less rally-driver than Hamish would've liked.

'Go help your mothers,' said Uncle Paul, slamming the door of the truck and striding into the house.

Hamish jumped out, heading in the opposite direction.

'Fuck that.' he said, beckoning me to follow.

'Aren't we meant to be helping?'

He wasn't impressed. 'You coming or not, fag?'

I followed, checking over my shoulder as we wandered across the paddock towards the trees.

I kept lookout while Hamish scanned the canopies. He spied a possum clinging to a branch only twenty feet up—unusual for this time of night. Hamish cocked his crossbow, but his bandaged hand was slipping on the stock. He cursed, put down the weapon and unravelled the bandage. The burn had healed well, but it still looked pretty grim to me—raw pink flesh outlined in dead skin, tobacco-brown from the iodine. Hamish couldn't have cared less about his injury. He picked up the crossbow, spun the tiller straight up at the creature and pulled the trigger. The whipcord twanged like a cello, aluminium sent climbing towards the lofts and spearing the animal in the shoulder, throwing it back. With flailing arms it fell through the branches like a marble in a game of Kerplunk. Hamish was delighted. We ran over. It was knocked for six but still breathing. Around its waist was a baby, clinging on for dear life, noticing the slack in its mother's embrace.

So that's why it didn't run away.

Hamish reached down and grabbed the end of the barbed arrow, tearing it from the possum's furry shoulder—dark crimson blood and the smell of fresh hide. Hamish reloaded.

'What are you doing?' I asked.

It'd be crueller to leave it like that, surely?

'What about the baby?'

He aimed at the baby's head and pulled the trigger. The bolt cut through the back of its skull with a dead thump, out through the eye and into the mother's heart. Hamish ripped the arrow from the carcasses, twizzling it round in his well hand. He turned and began walking back to the house, while I mourned the dead in the growing shadows, an insect orchestra clicking mid in the dusk.

Hamish called back. 'You gotta harden up.'

But I didn't want to harden up.

> Now HE was the kind of kid that would've thrown darts at sparrows! Except Hamish's skull wasn't empty. It was dangerously full. Better off without that stick of dynamite in your pocket.

The New Year party was people of the same ilk as my new family—well-mannered, serious white adults. There were a few other kids that Hamish knew from town as well, plus Frances and some of her friends. I avoided Hamish, focused on being the DJ for a tough crowd.

> You were knelt at the altar rifling through CD wallets when she floated over, intrigued and tapping a ringed middle finger on her drink, tucking blonde hair from turquoise eyes. Tanya was a peach. She wanted to know your next move as DJ, how you were going to win the room over. You were torn between satisfying or educating the masses—Grease Lightning or 1979. She loved 1979. She loved your accent too. She did a naff impersonation, dropping the T's and switching the vowels.

She laughed like sunshine and took a knee beside you, used your shoulder for support. The way she looked at you was just how you'd imagined it.

She asked me how old I was and I died a little inside. My saving grace was the thought of telling her I was fifteen now and then in five minutes it would be my birthday, so I could tell her I was sixteen.

'You going to school here?' she enquired.

I was due to start next week. It would've been eight months since I last went. She laughed when I told her because she thought I was joking, then got comfy in anticipation of me explaining myself, but I didn't know where to start, didn't want to talk about it really.

'Just cause—travelling and—just the way it worked out. Timewise I mean,' I scrabbled around. 'It's different over here too. Your summer is our winter and—I don't know. Just had to get away.'

Big plot holes, but man, who knew ambiguity could be so romantic? The vague approach was working. She was still there, flirting, asking if you'd come here to study.

'Come here to live.' I said. 'I live here now.'

'No way,' she said. 'That's choice!'

'Choice?' I raised an eyebrow.

Now it was your turn to make fun of her accent!

Cutlery tapped glass somewhere up around an F sharp. Uncle Paul wanted everyone's attention, pointed at me to turn the music down. He said some formal words strung in a logical order, went through the motions of thanking people for coming and guided their attention to the clock on the wall that was two minutes from a new year. People cheered, started moving around, forming a circle, linking hands. Mum was there with Aunt Kath. She looked young. Hair like wild flames parted past two bright emeralds. That morning, out of nowhere, she opened up the piano in the living room, took a deep breath and played a piece of music I'd never heard before, her farm-girl fingers transformed, sweet and delicate on the ivories. It was hypnotic. I didn't know what it was. I didn't even know she played the piano! Looking across the room on New Year's Eve I could sense the relief in her, see a real smile as she mingled through the party like a couturier's model.

Tanya placed her drink by the stereo, stood and grabbed my hands to stand with her, said we had to sing now.

'Choice.' I said.

Auld Lang Syne bellowed out—who knows what key. Hamish was on the other side of the circle, too wired inside to give a shit about complicated little me. He'd be fine without my friendship. I was glad to be moving out. When the cheering erupted at the end of the song, Mum came straight over and gathered me up. It took a second for the surprise to wane and for me to hug her back. She was never a hugger, but still it felt so familiar.

She wished me Happy New Year and Happy Birthday before being whisked away by the merriment.

Tanya tugged your hand, spun you back around, pressed her warm lips fleetingly against a blushing cheek, catching the corner of your smile.

'Happy New Year,' she said.

And looked you dead in the eyes.

'So. When are you sixteen?'

6
HAVE A CIGAR,
YOU'RE GONNA GO FAR

*Remember the Takapau Plains? Remember Rock FM
playing the whole of Shine On You Crazy Diamond?
Tanya got you into Pink Floyd. It was fate they played
it as you headed North to see her at Uni. You stiffened at
the thought, told yourself she was worth the wait. What
was seven more hours of virginity after all? Jesus. Just
think of what you passed up on man, and I don't mean
Mount Ruapehu. Think of Jade Baker and the knowing eyes she gave you when the wind blew her netball
skirt up. There's no such thing as the right time. I tried
telling you. Any longer and you'd have gone blind. This
road trip couldn't have come sooner—pun intended.*

Despite initial nerves I enjoyed my first year in a new
school. It was a blank slate in terms of my personality,
but I'd been more anxious than I'd hoped, found I didn't
quite have the guts to approach anyone. My initial secu-
rity blanket was to take obscure books into school and
make sure to be seen reading them, playing the mysterious foreigner.

*You missed a trick with those books. You might as well
have been reading them upside down.*

The success of entrancing Tanya had taught me to be vague and try to slip words in that showed off my Englishness. Keeping my words few was most welcome, coz I badly needed braces.

People-pleasers are known to lose their native tongue. Consider it method acting.

It was a small school, only a few hundred students. A big chunk of them were from China and Japan, boarding in dorms and keeping themselves to themselves. The rest were a mix of white or Maori that seemed to segregate with age. I didn't know why. Still, it was nothing like as volatile as my former school.

Rugby was the school's main focus—trying to find the nation's next Lomu. There were some genuine hulks kicking around the corridors, collars and shorts pulled up, stark tan lines on nut-cracking thighs. I'd grown lanky and thinned out. It would have been a waste of the nation's time to worry about my sporting potential. I had nothing to prove, no history in my new surrounds, so I was green-lit to go straight to the music department.

The music teacher, Mr Murdoch, had been in a rugby accident as a kid. As a result his neck had no tendons down one side and his head was permanently leant over. He gestured with his hands a lot when he spoke. It made him look like he was playing an invisible violin. The minute he found out I played guitar he was on to it, stuck me in a room with the like-minded Jethro Feck for me to show off to. Jethro was a great bass player and easily kept up. He was shy—not enough eye contact to decipher a colour, but a shag of brown fusilli hair. That lunchtime he brought his mates Colin and Campbell over. I was reading Jean-Paul Sartre's Nausea, drifting in and out of understanding.

> 'You have to choose—live or tell.' Slim pickin's but well done.

Colin was half Maori but bleached his shiny black locks thick peach. Campbell was pasty, greasy—a young Hen Broon. Behind them, Jethro bit his fingernails, like he'd bigged me up and was nervous I wouldn't meet expectations. Colin wanted to know how many Nirvana songs I knew, asked if I liked Weezer. Campbell asked me if I'd ever been in a band.

> Fuck yeah, you had! And can we not take a minute to reflect on the joy of the name Jethro Feck?

They were looking for a frontman and it was imperative they weren't a fan of Oasis. That was the reason for the interview, me being a Brit and all.

> The Gallaghers saved your carcass in England a bunch of times, man. How could you throw them under the bus like that? When Oasis hit big, even the jocks had time for music. You got left the fuck alone if you could crank out Wonderwall on request. And who can't do that?

75

They wanted to be called Dirk Sphincter and the Epitaphs.
I said I'd join if we could change the name.

*That was talentless Campbell's idea. The only good
thing he did was introduce you to NOFX and that whole
surf punk thing. That shit was hilarious! Jethro was a
sweetheart—wouldn't boo at a goose. Tasty bass player
too. Knew some ironic slap, thought Paul McCartney's
strap was too short, etc. And Colin, well, Colin was so
laid-back he could limbo under Miss Cullen's skirt if
he'd wanted. He was in the band for the craic of being
in a band, played a bit of rhythm and made you all look
cool. Smoked some weed too, right? Jesus! Amazing to
think you weren't tempted. And not a single fag since
take-off. On some kind of health kick? It can be done.*

I asked Mum for my songbooks, but they hadn't arrived
from England yet.

That's weird. The dogs had.

Part of me was actually relieved. Maybe I wasn't ready to
face the past yet. I started some new songbooks, wrote
goofy punk tunes without meaning and started piecing
together a set for the band. We'd decided on the name
Miss Demeanours.

*Be honest. That's not as good as Dirk Sphincter and
the Epitaphs.*

Elsewhere in school I got heaps of leeway. Teachers held my hand through the new system and other students wanted to help out the mysterious foreigner, see if there was anything worth getting to know behind the mask.

Perfect time to drop in another reminder of the lovely Jade Baker, Queen of the cherry poppers. There on a plate for you and willing to put more than just a decorative apple in her mouth. Her rep was sullied. It would've been a perfect introduction to your hindered sexual awakening—no strings, no commitment. What a frightened little possum you were.

Tanya had left to go back to Uni a week after we'd met. It'd been difficult to find privacy living with Aunt Kath and Uncle Paul over that Christmas, and I don't think Frances was best pleased her dorky cousin had stolen her friend away. Still, we'd managed a lot of first base stuff—kissing fully clothed with brief but miraculous wandering hands.

A little skin on the fingertips never hurt anyone.

The whirlwind spun me enough to hold out until next summer. I had plenty to focus on in the present—moving into a new house, starting a new school and so on.

Whatever.

Mine and Tanya's cross-country conversations racked up eye-watering phone bills. Mum made me get a job stacking shelves at Price Chopper on weekends to cover them.

77

Once my debts were paid, I stayed on and saved to get my driving licence. Aunt Kath had offered to pay but Mum said she didn't want to live her life like a charity, insisted I graft myself. Maybe she was being obstructive, rightfully nervous about youngsters hooning around the roads, but it didn't take too long to get my licence anyhow.

Mum had set up a dog-grooming business at home in town and barely needed the car, so it was pretty much mine—a burnt umber Sierra. Despite only living down the road from school, I drove in every day, pulling up outside the music department and taking my guitar out of the trunk in full view of as many students as possible. Mr Murdoch was there one morning, smiled and said I had my very own tour bus now.

Lightbulb!

Me and the band begged Mr Murdoch to let us use lunch-times to get on the road and tour other schools.

Yeah, the road!

We packed the gear and headed to the only lunch halls close enough—in Dannevirke or Woodville. If we felt lucky, maybe we'd push for the half-hour Palmerston North run. Their lunch hall was twice the size of the others. Wherever we went, we'd blast a half hour of comic fuzz then pack up and bolt back to Norseville, justifying our lateness to the other teachers with claims that it was for a project we were taking very seriously.

What was that song about the dyslexic fan of Bob Marley that built a shrine to Exodus from flexi-glass? Or the one about the guy with the arsehole for a belly-button that ate his parents? What planet were you on exactly? Even without marijuana!

Mr Murdoch entered us into a students' Battle of the Bands competition. I say competition, but we were the only ones in it, so of course we won. We were put in the running for the nationals, which would be televised on one of the three channels. We had to go meet the executives, but that's where the campaign ended. Our so-called punk attitude was just silly. We weren't what they were looking for.

That was Campbell's fault. Who let him do the talking?

I didn't mind. To be honest, I was relieved. As much fun as I'd been having, I was over the punk thing, couldn't keep up the façade any longer. My voice was frustratingly baritone for a punk band. I was suited to a more earnest timbre and ready to take music seriously again. Miss Demeanours had given me some well-needed confidence but I quit the band. Campbell did my head in and Jethro's parents were devout Presbyterians. When they heard us they said he had to stop playing with me. I was twisted and dangerous apparently.

Err...Revelations?

Colin and I stayed friends. He was funny as hell and always so high, always showing his perfect white teeth in an infectiously baked smile. He called me Braveheart and I ribbed him for his ludicrously un-native first name. I went to pick him up from his house once and his dad answered—a spherical mass of toffee flesh covered in tribal tattoos. The house stank of weed—a cross between cat piss and oregano. He was smoking a joint and offered it to me. I said I was driving, better not.

Something about that cat piss though.

Mum and I had been in our home eight months or so. It was bigger than our home in Cornwall but wooden and on waist-high stilts. She'd redecorated and no two rooms were the same. The lounge was half Indian restaurant, half granny flat. The kitchen was canary and blue-striped walls with loud plum polka dots on clementine doors. She'd become fascinated with new-age stuff, really digging into her pagan roots. Tacky trinkets and spell books sat on multi-coloured shelves, dreamcatchers and wind-pipes hung in doorways, porcelain wizards gawked at you from every angle.

Bless her. What a jumble sale. Her flare must've been bottled up for so long she probably just didn't know where to start. So it projectile vomited out of her! It was the design on the sofas that gave you hay fever, forget the continuous stream of dogs that were always around.

80

I searched the outhouse and the garage but couldn't find what I was looking for. I opened the loft latch and the heat came belching out. It was boiling up there. The air had been close and sticky all week—real earthquake weather. I tied my t-shirt round my face and ventured up, clawing through boxes at full speed to keep short the mission. Still nothing. Eventually, when Mum got home late, I asked her where my songbooks were. The books were full of things I knew would be painful to think about—things about Dad and other forgotten embarrassments—but I was ready to dive in and get some inspiration.

Mum was in the kitchen readying the dog bowls, surrounded by seven or eight mutts that knew dinner was imminent. She didn't hear me over their barking, their frantic claws on toadstool lino.

'Where are my books, Mum?'

She still didn't hear.

> Or pretended not to. Try speaking dog. She listens to them.

'Mum?' shouting. 'Where are my books?!'

She looked around. The dogs were getting impatient.

'What books?' she said sheepishly. 'Your songbooks? I didn't think you wanted those.'

> What the woof?

I asked her again and she repeated what I was afraid I'd already heard.

'Didn't want them?! Where are they? You mean you threw them out?!'

She wouldn't look at me, started filling the bowls to hush the dogs that snuffled at their supper. Normal volume resumed.

'Are you fucking serious? You threw them out?'

I didn't know what else to say. There were hundreds of ideas in those books, all too far away in my memory to recall without some kind of visual aid. Mum turned to look at me. She tried to hide it, but I could read the red-faced guilt.

Woofing hell!

I was starting to feel giddy.

'When did you get rid of them?' I said, gulping for air.

She stopped pouring the food and the remaining hungry dogs went ballistic. Over the noise of the barking, it sounded like she said 'England'.

Crying wasn't something I did but I could feel it brewing. I ran out of the house, a cross between livid and confused. I was trying to tell myself that maybe she was right. Maybe I didn't need them.

Regardless. Dick move. How's about you chuck those spell books out, Grotbags?

Mum and I had been through a lot, were as close as we'd ever been. She had a quiet wisdom and a dry wit, but like me never spoke about the past. It was words of encouragement in passing from her, a joke about our differences in tastes from me. I wanted to trust her, to believe that she'd had my best interests at heart. But my history had been thrown in the bin just as I'd finally found the courage to face it. I didn't know how to feel, my stomach in a sailor's knot.

Inside the house, the dogs were going ballistic again, but it sounded different this time. It wasn't the yaps of hungry mutts. It was primal, indigenous barking. Ten seconds later the earth began humming and a deep, unforgiving rumble knocked from the very depths of hell beneath my feet.

> *That is ridiculous. It was just a tremor! It lasted maybe five seconds.*

The earthquake sounded exactly like my fever dream from childhood.

> *You've not had that in years. And stop saying earthquake. It was a tremor.*

The humidity was making my skin tacky as I stared up at the stars in their millions.

> *Glass shards sparkling in eternity? Incorruptible hopes in God's own wilderness maybe? You can have that.*

Just like in the nightmare, the universe loomed mysteriously above—an ocean of pins and needles throbbing and threatening to make me sick.

I thought we'd established that was the vagina?

I tried to think of my lost books—the songs, the stories and salvations of the past—but it was no use. My history was an indecipherable fog—Dad in his study, Uncle Henry's ghost, Simon's dark eyes, Isaac's baritone.

They were gone.

My youth.

It was gone.

Jess.

Gone.

I found comfort where I always did, with the gospel of Dylan repeating in my head – It's easy to see without looking too far that not much is really sacred. It's alright Ma, I can make it.

What about 'Every day's been darkness since you been gone'?

With no tears I stared the universe in the face.

You mean you stared the vagina in the face?

I vowed to move on, stay well and live clean, focus on school and forgive Mum her misstep. I closed my hands in prayer and gave thanks.

Very nice, but wrong god this time, eh? Time for a brush with another one.

I'd stopped for gas in Taupo but was running low again as I reached Auckland to see Tanya at the end of term. I'd finished my exams and was in good spirits. Mum gave me $50 for doing so well, so I'd filled up and headed off.

Shame she didn't give you something more towards fixing your teeth. Or ask Aunt Kath? Paying your way is all well and good but, man, it was like a bomb had gone off in a graveyard. Braces too expensive and that medieval retainer could only do so much. I felt for you. At least you could take it out and shut your mouth. That was usually best.

Tanya's dorm was in the Newmarket district near the university. She lived with a couple of other girls, but they only shared the bathroom and kitchen. There was a lock on her door. She'd been sure to tell me that. She was waiting out on the street. It was late—well after midnight.

We're gonna let it all hang out.

She was in PJs, loose bottoms and singlet, fit and radiant as ever. I don't know what she saw in me, but I tried not to think about that. I guess through the distance and the shortened phone calls I'd retained some mystery maybe? Hadn't had time to overthink myself into being unattractive?

I pulled over, flashing my lights to get her attention. I took my retainer out as she ran and opened the driver's side, diving in to hug me. There was some fleeting eye contact to be sure it was me, then we were right back to the tonguing we'd left off from ten months ago.

You threw her a compliment. You could feel her chest— bare skin but for a layer of cotton turned amber in the streetlight. You couldn't wait to see if your imagination had been on point. Or points—pun intended.

Her room was thankfully dim, small and with lots of open books and lavender candles. Alice in Chains' Unplugged spilled out of a stereo, crawling around the walls on low, 'Heaven beside you, hell within'. We were straight onto the bed, still clothed and with her straddled on top. She had St Christopher on a slim gold chain hanging from her neck. It caught on my chin and tickled my nose. She laughed and spun the pendant to the back, lustfully exhaling and coming back for more.

She was a passionate, noisy kisser. Your mouth was dry from nerves but she kept you wet. She straightened up and stripped her singlet off. The aperture in your eyeballs sucked up enough candlelight to know your imagination had paled in comparison. You couldn't help but immediately put your hands on her peachy breasts, her nipples stiffening under your thumbs, waking against your clumsy caress. You sat up, tore your top off, your highland skin relishing a deceptive, warm hue. She put her hands down your pants, roughly fumbling a stiffy. You couldn't get your hands down her PJs—not without dislocating your wrists—so you rolled over, pulled her down on her back, her hands wrenching your dick painfully as they tried to let go.

The humidity made her heaving chest shine as she arched on her shoulder blades, fluttering eyes and crown in spin, St Christopher smothered, Layne Staley singing, 'If I could, would you?'

I swung my legs over the side and pulled my remaining clothes off, crawled back onto the bed ready to undress her.

You'd paid attention when you first poked your fingers around down there, knew every fleshy contour—brail to the blind. Now it was time for the visuals. Those PJs would've slipped off so easy. But wait...

'What are you doing?' asked Tanya.

I stopped in my tracks on all fours like a possum in the headlights, frozen by her question. My face was a foot above her crotch, my hands poised to disrobe her. I looked down at my naked body.

Four skinny limbs and a twitching prick.

'What do you mean?' I managed.

She was resting on her elbows. 'What are you doing?'

I had no answer.

She asked me if I believed in sex before marriage.

Believe?

I was flushed, suddenly exposed and mortified, confused and starting to droop.

She asked me again. Did I believe in sex before marriage?

Was the throbbing cock and birthday suit not a clue?

'Erm?' I said, still drooping. 'Do *you* believe in sex before marriage?'

She said she believed that God didn't want us to be sinful. She believed in purity and sanctity.

Flaccid.

I looked around for something to conceal my dignity, sat over the edge feeling utterly ashamed. She said we could still do other stuff, just not, y' know, all the way.

What are the rules?

I stuttered for a comeback, 'I suppose so, yeah. I mean... what are the rules? And what do you mean by *believe*?'

She was looking at me like I was a good kid caught up to no good and out of my depth. I continued.

'Isn't belief about confidence in the truth without proof that it's right? I mean, I don't go round *insisting* everyone has sex before marriage.'

> *Nice pillow talk Droopy Drawers. What were you waffling about? And why were you so easy on her? What sort of belief says you can have your cake but you can't eat it? Where in the Bible does it say keep your slacks on? People were always getting their dicks out back then. Adam and Eve had hundreds of kids! You shouldn't have rushed it. You should've stuck with the fingers a while longer. What's the difference anyway? Does she think God's looking in? Making sure it's the right kind of phallus? Digits only and heaven awaits? Nah, fuck that. Let no monster cast judgement.*

'You okay?' said Tanya, slipping her singlet back on and putting her arm around me, apologising for thinking we were on the same page. 'You know Frances is a Christian, right?'

I didn't. I deflated, but how could I get angry with her, even with my frustration.

> *Like this—FUUUUUUUUUUUUCK YOOOOOUUUUU!!!!*

Tanya would have to be the star in someone else's sky. She'd been a useful grail to covet, had kept me buoyant and focused, but I couldn't see me coming back from this. Humiliation was in the post ready to set my mind into overload, and I was already looking for some nice deep sand. She was out of my league anyway, on the straight and narrow. I was a non-believer, crooked toothed and crazy. I needed out, to reassess. She pulled my face around and kissed my lips but I didn't return the affection. I had a question.

'So that time you said it must've been amazing to see under the water when Moses parted the sea—that's not just a story? You believe that actually happened?'

'I believe in miracles.'

You not so sexy thing.

She was too close for comfort, gazing intently like she was trying to hypnotise me or something. She asked if I still wanted to see her.

'Umm...' I looked at the flower-shaped pillow concealing my dignity. What a ridiculous fig leaf.

'I feel like a bit of an idiot.'

She said I wasn't an idiot. I was sweet and funny and really grown-up.

I sighed at the condescension. 'So you want to get married?'

I was only half joking.

Desperate times.

I had nothing left to say. She did.

'You never talk about your dad.'

Neither did I want to. I tried to shrug it off, but she kept on, offering her ear and shoulder if needs be.

I narrowed my eyes, didn't know what she knew. Frances must've been talking to her about me. Telling her stuff about what happened to Dad.

A few beats went by as she stroked St Christopher, before offering me a slice of biblical wisdom.

Our present sufferings are not worth comparing with the glory that will be revealed in us. Yeah? That's very optimistic of you, Tanya. Where's the evidence?

'Faith in a truth without proof that it's right. Sorry, Tanya, I need to go.'

I threw off her arm and started pulling on my clothes, apologising like a stuck record. She was crying, saying I needed help, that *she* could help. I told her I didn't need it. I wasn't a charity, I just needed to wake up—literally and figuratively. I thought about lying and saying I had an interview I'd forgotten about but instead just repeated my false contrition.

You didn't owe her anything more.

I thought I should kiss her goodbye but she stepped away, said she was confused, worried. I said I was fine. She said she didn't believe me, called me a freak.

True colours.

I was out of there. I set off for home and prayed Rock FM would get me through the night.

Victim of Love. Don't You Cry. Lonely Boy. Ride a White Swan. Take Me to the River. Purple Haze. Cocaine. Helpless. Paranoid.

I made it home by dawn and my body shut down. I slept twelve hours, bookended by apocalyptic nightmares. I woke with a strange feeling that my soul was itching but my hands were mittens.

I walked to Price Chopper, needed sugar in my system. I bought a packet of biscuits and a litre of ginger beer, sat on a kerb and smashed the lot, belching with teeth full of syrup, carbonated eyes fizzing as I scanned around. The imaginary mittens came off and I was free to scratch again.

The supermarket was on the back streets of the main drag. Jade Baker lived in one of the houses round here.

Yes she did. And every boy with a whisker on his balls knew it.

I loitered, thinking maybe she'd show up, give away her position. I don't know what I thought I'd do, hadn't made a plan. I just wanted *something* to happen.

Sugar rush.

Then Colin's dad pulled up next to me in the car park. He rolled his podge out—flip-flops, tracksuit bottoms well below the belly, giant brown nipples sticking out the sides of a dirty vest, the whites of his eyes toked well and truly pink. He said hey and asked me what I was up to and if I'd heard the new Metallica album. I hadn't.

'Come see us sometime, bro. I'll hook y'up.'

He bought some beers, reminded me of the offer and drove off. I watched him pull away down Queen's Road towards the steelworks and, to my delight, I spotted Jade arriving at her house. I watched her go inside as my mind started vomiting fantasies at me, but just getting her to answer the door would give me something to hang on to. I started walking over, running some lines in my head and sniffing my armpits just in case. I stopped on the opposite side of the road, pausing to assess.

They said she was all woman.

I wrinkled my nose and shook my head, injected with a different kind of interest suddenly. I spun on my heels towards Colin's house. I didn't care about the new Metallica record. I hoped his dad would offer me a spliff. I wouldn't be saying no this time.

7 The Smallest Oceans Still Get Big, Big Waves

How much longer is this gonna take, you think? Coz you know there's a solution right here, don't you? It's that same solution you snorted before you started on this indulgent odyssey. The beauty of ketamine is that there's no hangover, man. You could come away from the window, put all this pain in a lead-lined box and dump it in the Thames. Just sayin'. You haven't found anything yet. Nothing to justify throwing in the towel.

I remember being stood outside Mr Stone's office.

Fuck's sake!

Colin was in there getting grilled for misbehaviour. It was my turn next. He came out with his usual indignant smile, gave me a high-five and skipped off down the corridor telling me to check out the fags in Mr Stone's shirt pocket when I went in.

The corridor was plastered with student's artwork, a staple-gunned mosaic of the brightest and best. Nothing of mine was up there. I'd given up on art. Having had a romantic vision of becoming an artist at the start of the year, I'd jacked it in after a few weeks with the teacher, Mrs Bevan—nice enough but on another planet and not exactly a well of inspiration. I was finding that with most teachers, in one way or another. School wasted precious time that could be spent doing anything else—including getting stoned of course.

Hamish's art was all over the walls. He was the year above but was allowed extra art classes with the younger students because of his talent. With my new hazy outlook on the world, I could step back and appreciate my cousin's wild output again—an electrical storm on a distant shore. He was so capable, he was going to go far whatever he did, expectations riding high. As artists go, I was amateur in comparison. Plus I didn't have the patience for long and thoughtful art projects. I spent most of my time making album covers and flirting with Jade Baker.

> *Jade. Back on the radar. She was dating Alex the Tool Bag but had plenty of room in her schedule for some adolescent teasing—leaning forwards over here, tits against you there. And let's be fair to Mrs Bevan for a second. Mister Bevan had just run off with another man. She spent most of her time munching overripe avocados and staring into the middle distance. Free pass to do fuck all as far as I'm concerned.*

I was over school. I was over dead-end Norseville. I couldn't wait for the year to be over so I could start saving over the summer to get out of there. Where? I didn't know yet.

What prehistoric school system makes you wear a uniform at seventeen? Compulsory shorts? Your chicken knees reminding you what not to wear out of school hours? Ridiculous. How were the little ones supposed to know they weren't allowed to talk to you? It was the right decision to wanna quit. Hey, I know. Let's chalk up your reasons for leaving one last time, just in case you get to the other side of this unnecessary recall with any regrets. Reason number one—nice and simple—the school uniform. See above. Reason number two—hopes of going to art school up in smoke. Quite literally. Reason number three—the test you took to determine your possible career options said teacher or religious leader. Not in your wildest dreams did you want that to happen. Should've walked out the gates there and then really.

It wasn't unusual for me and Colin to get summoned by teachers, but I had a feeling it was for different reasons. I was lazy and late whereas Colin was a real pain in the ass for them—disruptive and completely un-intimidated by the system that was writing him off day by day, happy to answer back and bask in the glory of my laughter if he was sent out. If I couldn't keep a straight face, I'd be swept up like an accomplice and told I was wasting my potential. I remember the laughter – lots and lots of giggles— but it's telling that I can't think of a single thing Colin actually said. I'm blaming the skunk.

No hang on, hang on. Wait a minute now. Let's think of something. Let's think of something funny that Colin said...

Nothing? Me Neither!

Mr Stone called me into his office. I had no idea why. English was about the only thing I was vaguely interested in anymore. He was weirdly pleased to see me— intrigued even—a rare grin under his brush. Still, I assumed I was there for a grilling and took up the position of guilty, perched on the edge of the seat ready to leave. He was a short, cartoonish man with cola-brown glasses too big for his face, wispy hair swept vaguely sideways. His token tweed jacket made you sweat just to look at. His short red tie screamed 'last minute'.

I'd always thought 'Mr Stone' was a character he had to play from nine to five. Whatever his first name was— that was his true identity. He wasn't much liked by the other pupils. He seemed pretty fair and forgiving to me.

In the bulge of his white shirt pocket, you could see the brand of his fags.

> *Twenty Red Royals for the head of English please. There were whispers of his wife leaving him and two kids he never saw. He made you read Narcissus and Goldmund as punishment for missing a deadline. Is that forgiving?*

He stared at me for a minute, tapping his pen on his leg as he sat back, figuring me out, one arm behind his head.

'I liked your story.'

He was talking about the one I submitted for mock exams. I didn't think it was anything special. I was probably stoned when I wrote it. It was something about a mother sending her two sons off to fight in the war—

one to the English and one to the German. I called it
An Interest in Successes on Both Sides. Mr Stone sat
forwards, serious.

'You did well. Eventually.'

I'd been late.

'Eighty-two per cent. That's an A,' he said.

'Is it?'

He said he'd like to see me carry that level into my final
exams. Said perhaps I needed to focus more. Perhaps
spend a little less time with my friends. I knew what he
meant.

*'That's an A!' His words. Perhaps you needed to focus
less!*

He gave me another compliment.

'I liked your song too.'

He was talking about the one I played in the talent
contest. It was a song I'd written about Tanya but it was
cryptic as all hell, no chance of meaning being exposed.

He asked me what it was called with his pen poised. It
was called The Organ Plays on Friday.

'The Organ Plays On Friday,' scribbling it down. 'Very
good.'

*You were the best thing about that talent show.
Certainly the only one that did anything original.
Should've won, but y' know, politics and what not.*

Mr Stone sat back in his seat again, switching character, hands back behind his head. The grilling didn't seem to be making an appearance.

'You write a lot of songs?'

I shifted in my seat and got comfy to answer.

'I don't know. Yeah?'

He asked me about my inspirations. I reeled off as many obscure names as I could think of—not because they inspired me particularly, but because I wanted to alienate him. He nodded along, pretending to know what I was talking about.

Still no mention of Guns N' Roses.

He asked me if I liked any old music. I said I knew some. Then it was his turn to reel off names and alienate me. I was surprised I was so in the dark, could only recognise a handful. He asked me if I knew Bob Dylan. I said of course. He chuckled and sat forwards again, formalising the meeting, snapping back into the role he was meant to be playing. He had a really distinctive laugh.

The truffle snuffler. Remember that laugh.

He wanted to read the lyrics to my song sometime, if it was okay? I was fine with that. I'd become paranoid about the idea that someone would steal my songbooks, so I hid all meaning behind various personalised codes. He wasn't going to penetrate that force field.

Mr Stone stood and gestured me towards the door. I obeyed.

One last thing before you go.

He asked if I knew Visions of Johanna. I stopped and turned around.

'It's Dylan,' he said.

'Probably then.'

'Little boy lost, he takes himself so seriously, brags of his misery, likes to live dangerously. I think you might appreciate it.'

The Lord moves in mysterious ways.

I scraped through my exams at the start of the summer and got to the holidays not caring about my grades, knowing that I wouldn't be going back.

> *It's worth remembering that you got zero per cent for your art project. Managing to blag a whole year of doing actually nothing was an art project in itself! One hundred per cent zero. Be proud.*

Mum didn't seem bothered about the idea of me leaving home, even though there was no plan beyond the leaving itself. She was a new-age hippie, opting for a laissez-faire attitude towards my future. She seemed happy enough and being left alone suited me just fine.

I got some labour work on the Blacks' farm, docking and castrating lambs, collecting and stacking hay bales. It was free time inside my head jogging behind the trailer in the dusk. My hay fever got pretty raw at times, my eyes streaming by the time I got home, but I was willing to put up with that for a job that was mindless and in the outdoors. It was all about saving for whatever I was going to do when I'd accrued some capital. That should only take a few months.

You're really racing through this chapter, aren't you? What you hiding from? Oh wait. I know. Go back.

Jade sidled up to me in class, said she needed a model for her art assignment on figures. She said I had a nice body, invited me over to her house.

Yeah why not, eh? Believing the hype just because! She'd borrowed a camera from Mrs Bevan and bought two rolls of film—one colour, one black and white. She hung some sheets up in her bedroom and pointed some lamps about. You stood there in your boxers trying not to get wood. She was using the black and white film first, which would help hide how pale you were. Basically see-through like a newborn fish. Jade was taking it all very seriously but that was for show. It was getting mighty hot in there. If only Jade's mum hadn't come home. She made her presence known for sure—licked her fingers and stubbed out the wick. Pun—well, pun in there somewhere! Jade threw you your t-shirt and flicked on the main light—game over.

'What about the colour film?' I said.
She looked disappointed.

A few moments of mystery. Did she want to bang? Or did she want to get some pictures? She did have a boyfriend after all—although she wasn't known for that being a barrier. I was gunning for the lust. I wanted to believe the smutty rumours. Good job you let your dick do the talking.

'I could do with some pictures for my project too, y'know? I was gonna get some magazines or something but, man, photos would be so much cooler.'

Her eyes twinkled. 'I can do that.'

Jackpot! A bold move justified and inspired by Boogie Nights I reckon. Who knew porn could be so arty? Jade tried to hide it, but that twinkle in her eyes had started life in the minge no question. Out to the car with a lamp in your hand and butterflies in your gut. Everything going smoothly. But uh-oh, guess what? Old fucking ditsy over there, wondering off in his head again. In the five-minute ride to your house, instead of thinking about how to make your move, you were thinking about your future as a photographer. You started as a perceptive, moody prodigy living in a high-rise studio overlooking New York, known for his tasteful nudes and enigmatic portraits of the homeless. Then you climbed the ladder, had Hollywood royalty queuing up to have their picture taken. The detail of having Jade as a former jealous muse was a hangover from your fantasies of being an artist—it was a nice touch, but why only a cameo? From there, you ventured into being an established director, invented some on set bust-ups, saw the

*premieres and heard the awards speeches, fell into a pool
at the after-show parties. So much unnecessary detail.
Got your priorities all fucked again, didn't you?!*

Back at the house, Mum was out, but it wouldn't have
mattered if she wasn't. Intrusion into each other's spaces
had never been an issue. Ever. I had a vague concern that
my covers were still on the floor by the stereo—and no
doubt a finished toilet roll lurking—but mainly I was
focused on trying to figure out how to use the camera,
unable to engage with what was actually happening in
front of me.

*Jade stripped to her knickers and lolled about on the
bed. You were free to have a good old gawk down the
lens at her milky skin and those two sweet jelly tots,
pubic spiders from the edge of black cotton.*

I didn't know where to begin making a move on her.
I switched interests rather than face any embarrassment
or rejection.

*Aperture? F-stop? Shutter speeds? The fuck are you
doing taking more interest in the camera than the tits
you're pointing it at? Fucking Boogie Nights.*

She had too much experience for the likes of me. Way
too up for it.

You asked her over!!

I hid a boner behind bent limbs trying to find the right angles and clicking away. It'd become a realistic idea that I'd stay on at school for the last year after all, get some freelance experience and take advantage of the supplies.

I took the roll of film from the camera as Jade got dressed, suddenly distant and embarrassed, eager to leave.

A few days later I went to collect the pictures, confident that whoever had developed them would see them as classy art rather than amateur porn. The sniggering clerk handed me a disappointingly thin envelope—nothing but blank negatives. I asked where the pictures were and he took great pleasure in telling me I'd underexposed everything. So, there weren't any!

> *Ha ha! A perceptive prodigy, eh? Too much dignity, not enough light! Good job we went through this though. Another mark on the tally of reasons to run away. Reason number four—failed, and I mean really failed, at being a photographer. You aborted that dream on the day of conception, you dumbass. That's alright. That's life. Photography is too expensive anyway. Do something that you already know about. Something that comes naturally. You fancy another line yet? How about a little smoke for the comedown?*

Jade got *her* photos back. I only ever got to see one of them. Her boyfriend Alex had found them and, after dumping her, he stole the ugliest one he could find, photocopied a bunch and stuck them up around the school halls, vandalising the student's art with my ghostly presence. In the picture, the flash had gone off, startling me into a white slab of hairless meat. I was caught in the middle of blinking and talking, my that'll-have-to-do teeth on full display. From then until the end of term, I heard giggles and whispers echoing through the corridors—a lofty addition to my ever-growing sense of paranoia.

> *You want to live in a town that remembers you for that? Didn't think so. Reason number five—humiliation past the point of no return. Thanks for that. Carry on.*

At the end of the long hard summer, I drove home from work one evening, past Drake's Bay and memories of Hamish leaping from the top of the cliff while I was skimming stones. I was able to smile and remember that dream-like summer spent following Hamish around like a happy lap dog.

It'd been a ten-hour day of labour on the farm and I was starving. I went to Price Chopper and bought my staple post-work meal of hotdog, Moro bar, vanilla slice, bag of lollies, bag of kettle chips and half a litre of ginger beer. I sat in the car and smashed the lot, licking hungrily at my sugary gums. Seventeen years of Mum's mince and tatties had taken its toll. I knew nothing about food and Mum had set no examples, had always been an uncomfortable cook. I loved being the boss of my own diet. One less thing to think about as far as I was concerned—munch the junk and get it over with.

I started rolling a cigarette for the drive home when there was a knock on my window. It was Mr Stone. I barely recognised him without his glasses. He looked like he'd just walked off a beach from the seventies. For some reason I instinctively threw my tobacco tin into the footwell before winding down the window, remembering halfway that I'd done pretty badly in my English exam.

'I hear you're leaving us?' he said.

He had that same nervous grin that looked like it was reserved for me.

'Hey, Mr Stone. Yeah. Bigger fish to fry or something.'

'If you're leaving, you don't have to call me Mr Stone any more.'

He reached his hand out. I supposed I should shake it.

'Please. Call me Arthur.'

He asked me what my plan was, but I didn't have an answer. I'd appreciated his belief in me and felt I owed him though.

'Sorry I messed up my exam and all. I should've done better.'

He waved his hand insistently, said he wasn't Mr Stone, that was just a role he played.

You were right!

He said my talent was obvious and that school wasn't for everyone. He said I'd succeed wherever I went.

And up went the pedestal.

'You got a minute? You want to see something?'

I couldn't think of a reason why not. I got out and followed him across the car park. He jumped into his tan car and reached across to unlock the passenger side. The mustard door creaked and I slid in. We drove back onto the main road and headed North away from the gorge, Ry Cooder on the tape deck. We took a right up a track that took us to the top of the town and pulled into a layby. He jumped out and gestured me to follow, hopping over an iron gate to a proud field that overlooked the whole of Norseville, lit only by the burgundy sunset. I could make out a tiny silhouette of Uncle Paul and Aunt Kath's castle. Mr Stone stood by my side as we gazed upon the world.

Arthur.

He asked me to look in particular at the ruts in the earth, where every few hundred metres the ground seemed to shunt itself upwards. There were five or six consecutive plateaus before rolling acres of farm took up the slack and disappeared into the mountains.

'You see that?' he said. 'Earthquakes.'

Apparently when the Europeans arrived in the 1870s, there were only a few of those ruts. The land used to be much flatter and with more trees. The explorers set up camp by the forest that was known as The Eighty-mile Bush, which they then dismantled to sell the wood to the railroad companies. That was why Norseville was known as a sleeper town, but I could think of some other reasons. The new inhabitants paid homage to the Norse gods by naming the town somewhat unimaginatively, and moved the wharenui ten miles west. I'd been follow-ing okay until he said 'wharenui'. He could tell I didn't know what that was, so I thought I may as well ask.

A wharenui was a traditional meeting house. A place of community for Maori.

'So, can you tell me what Waitangi Day is?' Mr Stone replacing Arthur for a moment.

'Isn't that when the whites got the natives drunk and made them sign all the land over?'

He snuffled his distinct chuckle.

'Something like that!'

His take on Waitangi was that for the whites it was a day of celebration, symbolising frontier and the founding of a new world. For Maori it was a day of reflection and a podium for injustice, a chance to remind the world of their hoodwinked ancestors.

Is this going anywhere?

He was saying life was bigger than all of us. That whoever we were, whatever we believed in, we were always and forever at the mercy of something we couldn't control. He said to forget caring what other people thought because when the universe was ready, it would shunt us out of kilter without warning – just like the ruts that stretched out before us.

'Follow your heart, son,' he said, tapping his shirt by the Red Royals that said hi from his pocket.

Hello.

We stood silent. I think I understood. He seemed to be saying that nothing we do matters, but that we should do it anyway, and with vigour.

Sounded to me like he was trying to get rid of you.

'You read that book I gave you? Hermann Hesse?'

It had a good cover.

I recited the only lines I could remember.
'Full of secrets, life stared at him, a murky unfathomable world, an impenetrable thorny forest full of fabulous perils.'
He smiled proudly and put his hand on my shoulder.
'There's a Maori proverb,' he said. 'Ka mate kāinga tahi, ka ora kāinga rua. It means—when one house dies, another house lives.'

That was exhausting.

We headed back to town. He drove straight past the car park where we'd hooked up. I thought maybe he wanted to show me something else. I was thinking about the mess of tobacco in my footwell and having to sift through the chocolate wrappers and greasy paper bags to save it. He pulled up outside my house—I didn't think to ask how he knew where I lived, just reminded him that my car was down at Price Chopper. He chirped that laugh again, turned back up the street and made the drop-off, hoping he'd see me again before I went wherever I was going.
I made a cigarette from tobacco, dry mud and fluff before driving myself home and crashing out on the floor by the stereo, still not sick of No Code.

Habit.

Dusk on the farm, late January 1999, and I was hosing sheep's blood down the slaughterhouse drain with Kingi, the head labourer. He was proudly showing me the eel he'd speared for his supper. It was dead slime coiled in a bucket to me. No amount of sugar could make that palatable.

Across the paddock, Mr Black—the boss man—came speeding through the evening mist, headlights only just necessary. He pulled up next to us as we stood vaguely to attention.

'Jump on. We gotta go!'

There'd been an accident. It was Hamish.

I jumped on and we sped off towards the farmhouse where I was parked. He told me what he knew.

Hamish had been racing his dad's car along Knight's Road. A possum had run out and he'd swerved to avoid it, gone through the barrier flying down the bank, rolling the vehicle twice and ending up in the river.

Hands up who thinks Hamish was trying to hit that possum?

He was in hospital, critical condition. Aunt Kath and Uncle Paul were there but no one had told Mum yet. She wasn't answering the phone. I was to go home and track her down, then get us to the emergency ward, quick as possible.

There was a car parked in the middle of the drive. I hadn't expected to see it. I jumped as I dodged by in the dark. It seemed familiar.

Tan? With a mustard door?

I went in through the back. All the lights were off apart from Mum's bedroom at the end of the hall. My mind was playing catch-up through the adrenaline. If she's home, why isn't she answering the phone? I tip-toed up the hallway as something unnerved me.

There it is! The truffle snuffler!

I approached Mum's door, ignoring the unwritten rules about space invasion.

What a stupid laugh.

The phone in the kitchen started ringing as I flung Mum's door open.

Ewwwww.

Mum and Mr Stone froze half naked at the end of the bed. I could tell it was the aftermath by the guilt on their faces, the state of the covers and what I assumed was the musty smell of middle-aged sex.

The phone was still ringing.

I imagined the relative minor as I stared at the busted lovers, all of us tranquilised and unable to speak. The phone wasn't stopping.

> *For god's sake, answer it. Get that gross old turtle sex out of your head!*

Wide-eyed, I turned up the hallway. Mum was trying to explain herself, her footsteps thudding after me on a floor with no foundations.

I got to the phone. It was Aunt Kath. Hamish was dead.

> *Reasons numbers six, seven, eight, nine and ten.*

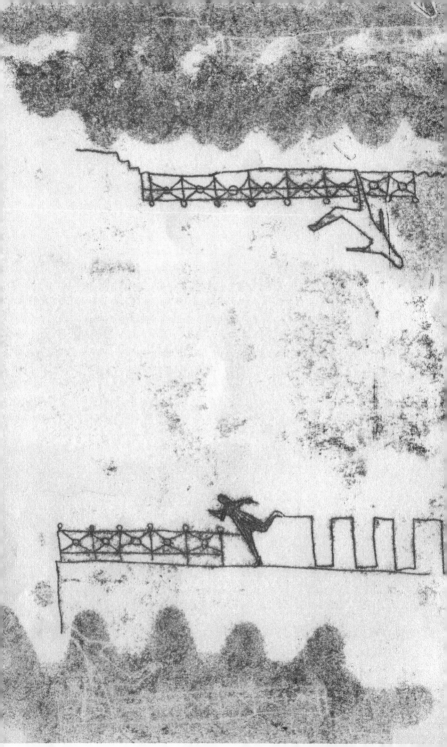

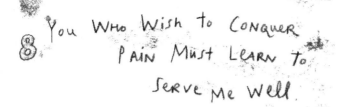

8. You Who Wish to Conquer Pain Must Learn to Serve Me Well.

I remember crying for the first time since I was a kid—a mirage of tears on desert cheeks.

I'd innocently followed the crowds and found myself in the Vincent Van Gogh Museum in Amsterdam. The penniless madman we learnt about at school had always seemed grunge to me—one of life's introverts tripping from one shitty hand to the next, his work his sanctuary. I switched off from caring about him when I learnt that he took the coward's route and shot himself though. Suicide had lost its romance somewhat since...

Since when?

Still, I'd been in good spirits.

Thought not.

I was willing to ignore my moral judgement of Vincent to kill some hours looking at the man's work. Following his timeline was easy on my tired eyes, whole chapters of his life summed up in bite-sized quotes. Things like, 'Lives with his parents. Mainly draws' and 'A peasant painting should smell like bacon.' That made me smile.

I love bacon. For his Sunflowers masterpiece, he said he had to dig as deep as he'd ever been in order for it to 'sufficiently catch fire'—and still it never sold!

Maybe last night's haze had softened me up but I had a strong sensation I wanted to be his friend. I'd tell him that I'd have bought his paintings even if no one else did. I'd tell his art dealer brother to do more. I'd forgive him for how he ended his life. I thought about Kurt Cobain and Something In The Way popped into my head.

As I rounded the corner on the home stretch of Vincent's story—his mind struggling and sickness taking over—the painting on the wall in front did something to me. A present for his nephew Willem, it was unlike anything else in the gallery—no yolk yellows or bacon browns. It was glorious, completely unexpected. It was like I'd never seen blue before. My jaw dropped and I was hypnotised. Tears began gathering at the derelict lock behind my eyes. I suddenly sobered, alone and exposed by Vincent's Almond Blossom, bled onto the canvas from the soul of someone desperately trying to connect the dots of the universe. I couldn't contain it. I wept, regressed to the blubbers of infancy. I didn't know what to do.

> *Lives with Gauguin. Cuts off his ear. Guy was a nut job. How is this the first thing that springs to mind from your time in Amsterdam? Far more to get stuck into than your sudden blubbering. Stop cherry-picking!*

Before I left New Zealand for good, I made some demos at the Stomach studios in Palmerston North, my entirely simple plan being to move to London and make my fortune as a rock star. One of the songs was called Anybody But Yourself, written after seeing Hamish's body in the casket—a bloated, rubbery alien. There were no tears from me though.

How did that one go again? I can remember the words but the melody escapes me.

Hamish had been sent off routinely and without incident—the last thing he would've wanted. I stood on my own at the back of the church, gritting my teeth at the religious platitudes. Uncle Paul's face looked serious as always, but the cogs in his brain had definitely softened. He loved his boy, just had a funny way of showing it.

As the procession filed out, I stayed facing forwards in defiance, thinking I must be the only one that really knew Hamish. I watched the reverend's apprentice pull the curtain around the casket. It snagged and another boy had to help, stifling their childish laughter to uphold the solemnity. I sighed but I didn't cry.

A power cut
And your body on the shelf
An unfamiliar stillness
Anybody but yourself

Tanya walked past with the procession and glared at me, rolled wet eyes and shook her head.

That's what a year of ignoring her will get you.

I muttered sarcastically under my breath that she wasn't being very Christian. She stopped and collared me, her clean breath tickling my ear as she told me to go to hell.

Point proven.

When Mum dropped me at the airport, we shared something of a hug but our minds were on different pages—had been since I caught her with her lover, Mr Stone.

Let's not think about that again.

I was still angry. She seemed relieved I was going, which only made me angrier. Definitely no tears from me.

I planned to wipe the memory of New Zealand by the time I reached England. I had two stopovers before then. The first hurdle was a forty-eight-hour glitch in Denpasar.

You don't need to go through the Denpasar debacle surely? You'll only kid yourself that you were the victim somehow, not just an ignorant westerner duped into handing over wad after wad of money to whoever saw you coming—which was everyone.

It was late when I landed. I didn't know I'd be arriving on Nyepi. A national day of silence.

What were the chances of that? No electricity? Your taxi couldn't even turn its lights on! No wonder your

*arse was twitching, bruising through an inch of sponge,
thrown around like sweaty livestock. On your way to
an abattoir in the Amazon for all you knew.*

The white-knuckle ride came to an end and cost me
an amount in a currency I hadn't had time to compute
before the taxi disappeared into the night. I was shaking
and my squinting eyes were stung with sweat. I couldn't
see the hotel I'd been taken to or the short, grumpy hotelier that led me to my room with a nine-vault torch. I was
told I wasn't allowed to use the lights until morning and
he shuffled out. The only clue to my surroundings was
the smell—which didn't paint the prettiest picture.

*The smell and the sound. That was the giveaway. I'm
going with brothel.*

I sat on the bed listening to what sounded like a
record-breaking rally in a furious mixed doubles match.
When the rally ended, it sounded like everyone had won
something.

New balls, please.

An hour or so later, the hotelier, whose face I still hadn't
seen in any detail, came knocking with his torch. He
pushed straight past me with a neon-bikini-clad line of
young girls in in tow.

You're sure they were girls?

He lit them up—spidery eyelashes crawled across the ceiling, their plasticine faces moulded into empty smiles. I felt sick and said no thank you, but the man didn't like that. What he lacked in English vocabulary he made up for in volume. So I tried to mime that I was too tired, but he didn't like that either. I'd wasted his time, which was precious and cost money. I paid to get him out so I could be terrified in solitude. Then he shouted at the girls and led them away. There was no sign of emotion from any of them.

> *Did you want them to look disappointed? See you as the tourist who's not like all the others? A saviour that slipped through their fingers. Please. A wasted opportunity is what that was. I'll forgive your refusal because they couldn't have been older than fifteen and likely had penises.*

Exhaustion put me to sleep, but only for a few hours. When the sun finally came up, I had blood all down my face, the pillow like a Rorschach test. I must've had a nose bleed.

> *That was one hell of a nightmare! But, look, can we get past this? It's just you being calamitous in a world you don't belong in. Yes, you had a strange and shitty time, but it was hardly Midnight Express. Oh, Billy! Get back to the airport and calm the fuck down. Oh, err, what did you do with your first days of liberty? Sat in a departure lounge staring at the board like a puppy at the front door. Not your finest moment. Let's forget it.*

I didn't get jelly-belly, but the Denpasar debacle scared the shit out of me anyway. In the departure lounge I bought a book from a donation table, then sat on top of my bags and waited.

The book I'd bought had had its front cover ripped off at some point and replaced with an age '5' birthday card sellotaped to the spine. In biro above the '5', it said 'Slaughterhouse'. I had no idea what it was about. I chose it coz it made me laugh for the first time in a while. On the back cover it sounded like it would be a memoir of some kind—something about a prisoner of war that witnessed the bombing of Dresden, but as I started reading, it was far from that. Before Billy Pilgrim is even taken prisoner, as he leans on a tree in Luxembourg, he becomes unstuck in time. He can now time travel and see all points of his life before, during and after the war. His memories become an inseparable cycle of lucid vignettes, leading him inevitably to Dresden and the needless destruction of it. He also gets abducted by little green aliens and taken to be studied in a space zoo. This wasn't a book about the war! But what was weird, was that it wasn't weird at all. The aliens and the time travel were far less ridiculous than the mindless massacre of a city that posed no threat to anyone.

I forgot all about my barely lamentable holiday from hell.

> *You thought about how you could use misery the way he did. You thought about how much you wanted to be around when something catastrophic happened. Tragedy certainly is compelling.*

I'd smacked my shins on the first hurdle leaving home, but I had no alternative but to try and shake off the limp. I was meant to be aiming for London, freedom, stardom, with one more stopover in Amsterdam for a night on my own in the city. On the plane from Indonesia, I started to worry I'd made a terrible mistake, that what I needed was to stop and assess before going any further. Maybe thirty-six hours of thinking time in Amsterdam airport would do it? Stay put. No rash decisions.

Boring!

But then something pulled me out of my anxiety descending over rainbows of tulips in the spring sunshine. I suddenly wanted to prove something to myself, lured by some kind of romantic vision or expectation I had of the city.

I'm only ever trying to help. Couldn't have you bailing after one mishap. The smell of freedom was even stronger than the smell of weed.

My parents had met in Amsterdam. It felt familiar somehow—the root of everything I was trying to forget. I wanted to stand up to it, brush it off as some petty chapter I could forget. I wanted to hold my head high and strut the streets of the city with no hand to hold, give the finger to my history, chalk a new fate on a clean slate. I wanted to stand in the foyer of the Theatre Carré, where my parents had met, imagine their doe eyes glazing over as they jumped into a life they'd take a big shit on and then hand down to me.

I think it's pronounced Carr-eh?

I wanted to think about Leonard Cohen's prose, of Mum and her naive desperation, of young Dad unsuspecting of his destiny on cloud fuck-up. I wanted to stand there and be unimpressed, tell myself that their history wasn't my future, break the curse and find closure once and for all.

First things first.

It never happened.

It didn't need to.

I got stoned in the first Koffieshop I entered, and left in such a fog I could barely see my own ample nose, let alone the Theatre Carré. The layout of the city made it impossible to get lost geographically but as mind sets go, I was nowhere to be found. I don't remember much else.

> *Allow me. You wandered the cobbles with a coat-hanger smile and couldn't believe this was living. Everyone smiled back and spoke English. You fell into a pub but got hauled up for skinning up on the bar. No dramas. Worrying that you looked like a loser, you ordered your first beer instead. I was so proud.*

I'd never taken to beer—didn't like the taste as much as anything. And I'd always been anxious around it for obvious reasons.

You're not like your dad though, are you? Only one way to find out.

The taste played no part if I skulled it back and gave no time for it to sit on my taste buds. Fizzy, fast and fresh. Ten minutes later my legs tingled and I wanted to find somewhere to have another smoke.

It's coming back now, right? Smoke, drink, wander. Such confidence I'd never seen in you. Red lights up as the sun goes down, thirsty boy. No kid likes beer, even if they say they do. You're a man now and the terrain ahead is a man's terrain. You need a man's fuel. Seems you're not like your dad. See how happy you were. He never looked happy. Had it all wrong. You, sir, are a natural. Now go spill your guts in the canal and get some grease in your belly.

I don't know how or what time I got back to my body-odorous-budget hostel, but I woke up at early o'clock, my liver finally getting a chance to deal with the sugar. Despite the dry sick on my jacket and a bloody knuckle, I felt great.

Your first hangover. Pretty sweet, right? Reflective.

I hadn't made it to the Theatre Carré to purge my history, but now I felt like it didn't matter. I didn't care. Any anger I had was buried.

By a potion you can get on tap.

At that moment I didn't need anyone but myself. There was no shrine to keep pretending to. The curse had been lifted.

Finally! Let's get out of here. Another kind of big smoke awaits.

I wasn't ready to go to the airport.

Fair enough. Full English please. A couple of hours of downtime. Coffee with a 'c'? Knew you'd like it.

I wandered the cobbles, chipper and aimless. Tourists took pictures of those they loved and I skipped like a ghost among them—a blurry signature in the cherished memories of others. I was already thinking about the next time I'd have a drink and how I'd manage my tolerance to avoid throwing up.

Something about that oblivion though.

I had time to do something cultural before I went to the airport, so I lit a cigarette and opened my eyes to what was around, followed Amsterdam's daytime tourists.

I found Van Gogh, the Almond Blossom and the first tears I'd wept in far too long.

Get on that fucking plane!

YOU WHO ARE SO GOOD
WITH WORDS AND AT
KEEPING THINGS VAGUE

The dream begins with an interview in the stockroom of a record shop. Some hippy chick is listing album titles. All you have to do is say who made it. Tell you what, I'll play the girl. Psychocandy?

I wondered how many different ways I could say I don't know.

'Not sure.'

Three Feet High and Rising?

'Is that the band?'

No, that's the title of the album. You know who that is?

'What? Psychocandy?'

Do you need me to explain the exercise again?

'You say the album, I say the artist?'

Artist or band.

'Or band. Of course. Right. Go.'

Warsaw?

'Haven't heard that one.'

Cosmo's Factory?

'Is that the band?'
 She closed her Camden-blue eyelids.

I say the album, you say the band.

'Band or artist.'

Just breaking character here for a second to say nice one for that. Made it one–all in my books. Back to the interview.
Music for the Masses?

'Oh, who's that again?'

Electric Warrior?

'That rings a bell.'

Crooked Rain?

'When was that made?'

The Chronic?

'Can't remember.'

Rumours?

'Led Zeppelin?'

No, that's Fleetwood Mac. Quite a big record that one.

'Maybe they didn't have it in New Zealand.'

Really?

'JJ Cale!'

Again, breaking character—bonus point for you there.

It was a train wreck. When I tried to explain I was into real music—not modern or electronic stuff—she shook her head, looked baffled, like my excuses were so dumb they didn't deserve a response. Then I told her I was in London because I was a singer—this job was to tide me over. She laughed and said I needed to open my mind, but thanked me for my honesty. She said she didn't need a singer, she needed someone that knew about music to buy and sell records for her shop.

> *Can't wait to see her face when your album goes gold. You don't want to work in Camden anyway. Way too cliquey.*

I thought I *did* know about music. Confused, I thanked her and walked out into London's congested, sniggering bustle.

Actually, you called her a dick under your breath. Or was that me?

I'd been devouring my savings at a Travelodge while I scouted the city trying to locate the record labels I'd be visiting to let them know there was a new talent in town. But the city was like an Escher. I couldn't wrap my head around the public transport so I just bought an all-zones travel card every day, adding to my financial depletion and giving me no sense of geography. I'd get lost and frustrated so give up and go back to my room, another day wasted. I ate fried chicken and ginger cake with a beer every night. After a couple of weeks, necessity shoved me outside to find work and a place to stay. I bagged the interview at the record shop and assumed I'd get the job so didn't look for anything else. I suppose it was good fortune running into Dice when I did.

Good fortune? It was a bloody miracle.

I met Dice in the first renting agency I went to. He looked like a rebellious Hanson brother, didn't look like he should be working there at all.

You've had time to think of that analogy. What you actually thought was how much you wished you looked

like him—spotless skin, long blonde hair, eyes the
depth and colour of a plunge pool.

Dice asked me why I was in London and laughed when I told him. He wasn't laughing *at* me, it was that he'd done the same a few years back, had had the same dream, played guitar and wrote songs himself. Formal bore about income and background checks went out the window as he told me about his career of near misses. Then the subject moved delightfully to the songs of Bob Dylan. We both agreed that Idiot Wind made divorce seem like a good idea. He sat back and perused me with a twinkle in his eye.

'You've got a little twang in your accent?' he said.

I'd never had a full blown Kiwi accent, but I slipped in and out of the odd vowel here and there. The trusted icebreaker never failing.

Keep it vague, keep it cool.

'Bit of Kiwi in there. Did some time down under.'

Dice smiled. 'I've got a break in five minutes. You smoke?'

'Sure.'

I waited on the street thinking how little London was like I'd imagined. It was dirty and exclusive, busy but lacking community. I didn't want to talk to anyone and it seemed no one wanted to talk to me either. Dice came out wearing Indiana Jones's leather jacket. He was cool and confident, rattling off his pitch.

'Yeah, bollocks to getting stuck in the system, mate. You want a room? I've got one you can have.'

Boom!

'Can you pay cash though? It has to be cash. It's a council flat but I'm never there. I'm staying at my girlfriend's across town. She's a DJ. The first female in house. But yeah, the room's empty, I just need to know if you're interested. Got someone else that wants it actually, but he doesn't listen to Dylan. What you thinking?'

'How much is the rent?'

'We'll figure that out.' He smiled, shaking my hand. 'It just has to be cash. But no bills. Apart from the phone.'

I had no one to call.

He sketched out suddenly, looking up and down the street on tiptoes.

'Where is it?' I said, bringing him back to earth.

'Cromwell's Estate. Zone 2, SE8. Where they filmed Nil By Mouth. There's two rooms and you can have the one on the left. Living room, bathroom, kitchen—all there to be used. Bathroom sink is blocked. Need to get someone round for that. You can clean your teeth in the bath though, right? Just kidding. Although you will have to do that, so—not just kidding! Need to get someone round for that. I come home sometimes, but you'll have the place to yourself mostly. Listen to the records, watch the videos, it's all good. I'll call in tomorrow and you can pay me the first month coz I got to go away. No deposit or nothing. But cash. It has to be cash. Here.'

He reached inside his jacket and pulled out a plastic fob key.

Saint Dice. You'd have been on the streets if not for him. He gave you the keys to his home based on your knowledge of Dylan!

It really was a miracle. Needless to say I bit his hand off.

Carrying my life across the city, I got off at the wrong stop and must've walked two or three miles before I finally got there, sweating buckets and gazing skywards at Daubeney Tower. It lurched out of the ground like Carrie's hand, surrounded by five-storey gravestones. I was disappointed. It was a little too hostile for my farm-boy sensibilities.

What were you expecting? Nil By Mouth's got Ray Winstone in it.

The flat was unloved and pretty much bare, the bathroom sink filled with a stagnant grey soup and the kitchen coloured in stale nicotine, stocked like Old Mother Hubbard's. In the living room there was a tonne of videos and records housed on plank shelves, a state of the art TV, VHS and brand new hi-fi, all at odds with the rest of the flat. My room was just a bed on a bare floor, steel tacks around the perimeter where once lay carpet.

Sorry your majesty but beggars can't be choosers. Unloved, yes, but perfect. You didn't need to pay attention to the interior anyway. It was twenty-four storeys

*high. The view was spectacular! And Dice had all the
records you needed to educate yourself—'open your
mind'. He would've nailed that interview.*

I celebrated my first night in a new home listening to
Psychocandy with a six-pack. I managed four before I
had to hang my head over the toilet and go to bed. There
were no curtains and the city twinkled below.

The next day I paid Dice the last of my savings for the
first month. He said he knew I was cool. He could tell.

'You're a Capricorn aren't you? Early. Like third or
fourth of January?'

'January the first!' I told him, somewhat amazed. 'How
did you know that?'

'You're the same as me,' he said, pumping his fist.
'Capricorn through and through.'

He was going to be away for a bit, but he had some
contacts at record labels and would sort me out with a
plan when he got back in a month, become my manager.

Your very own Albert Grossman. But better looking.

I sent a letter to Mum with nothing but my whereabouts
on it. It felt cold, but I let it pass.

You deserve a drink.

I'd wanted to be the musical version of Tarantino, working in a video shop while he wrote his movies, but no
record shop would take me on. The only job I could find

was stacking shelves at a supermarket forty minutes away. I was gutted. It hardly adhered to the dream.

> *You of all people should know that dreams are malleable. You just have to adapt—incorporate the treadmill on the bottom rung. No dramas.*

I made no connections at work. The hours were long and unsociable, but the solitude was ripe for many a brain voyage into my idealised future. I could work 'shitty job' into the narrative I was working on. It gave the rags-to-riches element some authenticity.

> *Not quite a prisoner of war but we'll take it for now, eh, Billy Pilgrim?*

The record labels would have to wait, but that was okay, Dice was going to sort me out. I could work my way through his records and write more songs in the meantime.

Weeks rolled by. I wanted to be busier but I didn't know how, and London was a labyrinth worthy of a Goblin King.

> *Turn back, Sarah!*

Whenever I ventured out I couldn't wait to get home, something always nagging at me to be alone.

> *Who said solitude is the path over which destiny, something, something? Some clever twat. It's something*

about solitude showing you who you really are. Chin up.
Kurt Cobain was sleeping in his car the night Never-
mind *came out.*

I wished I could see more of my new and only friend.
He popped by sometimes to collect the rent, and it was
welcome relief from isolation. He'd quit his job at the
renting agency, said the boss was a Nazi. I asked him
what he was doing for money.

'I find ways. Got a lodger now too.'

He flicked my arm jovially with the back of his hand.
There was something familiar about him, but I hadn't
been able to place it.

Sometimes we'd go to the Goose and Granite down
the road for a drink and a yap. The pub was pretty grim,
the locals glued to their stools and the landlord always
swearing at the fruit machine the same way he swore
at his wife. I made sure to lose the Kiwi accent when we
were in there. Didn't want to break the ice with any of
those gargoyles. It was easy enough to find a quiet corner
or play pool, zone the rest of society out. Dice could talk
for England, had an encyclopaedic knowledge of movies
and music, and continued to throw anecdotes of his time
in the industry my way. He'd come close, he reckoned,
but ultimately decided they were all a bunch of assholes
that didn't deserve what he was offering. He could help
me though. Knew the pitfalls. He was getting in touch
with some of his old contacts but warned me that the
industry was painfully slow. I should just work on my
songs in the meantime and keep writing. The thing I

needed most was patience. I said it was hanging on by the skin of my yellow teeth.

'There's a lyric!' he cheered, clinking my glass.

Something occurred to me. 'You know you haven't even heard my demo yet?'

He sank his pint. 'Let's do it! Just gotta get something. Meet you back at mine.'

Half an hour later, back at the flat, and Dice rolled in.

'You smoke weed?' he said. 'Course you do. Capricorn!'

I played him the tape and we got baked. He quite liked the songs but they didn't blow him away. He said there was something of a cross between Elliott Smith and Nick Drake in there—neither of whom I'd heard of so didn't know what to take from it. All I could think was that I needed more.

Dice said he could help me with some recording equipment—knew a guy that knew a guy and what not. I indulged him in my philosophy about what matters most creatively—integrity, unpredictability, legacy. I told him I wanted to be around in fifty years, not a flash in the pan.

'I want to invent the wheel not make tyres!' I said.

We high-fived. Our doe eyes puffy and pink.

A few tweaks and you've got your first anecdote.

The next time Dice came round, he brought a four-track recorder, some cables and a microphone. They looked brand new. He showed me how to use it all and said he'd see me in a month or so. Then, like Keyser Söze, he was gone again.

141

Poof!

I found Dice's Elliott Smith albums and went deep. If there was a similarity, it was in the breathy voice. But where Smith had soul, mine was just weak. He was so much better than me. His melodies so satisfying—full of surprises, but never jarring. I went back to the shelf-stacking, but at least I had something to keep my creativity occupied, trying to put my musical education into practice. More weeks went by. I hadn't written a hit single, but I could drink four cans without having to hang my head over the toilet.

That's an achievement. Incremental steps, dear boy.

That saying about how time flies when you're having fun? Well, it flies when you're doing fuck all as well! Enough was enough, I couldn't wait around any longer, so thought I'd at least try and get a gig somewhere.

I'd written a couple of songs about London and thought they'd connect, inspired after finally watching Nil By Mouth. Oddly, the first time I watched it, the violence and drug abuse went over my head. I was so focused on the soundtrack. Clapton's weeping twelve-bar and the scene with the girl singing Marilyn Monroe transcended the brutality somehow, made it a thing of elegance. And the scene with the nan singing Can't Help Loving That Man of Mine was filmed in the Goose and Granite according to Dice. Walking home from work one night, I saw that they were holding an open mic at the weekend. I found courage enough to talk myself into it.

Two cans equal courage.

I wandered down to the pub, imagining the rapturous applause and the buzz that would start circling immediately after my set, the chance that someone with connections would see me and invite me towards the dotted line.

It was pretty empty in there, the usual locals rooted firmly in place. They made up about half the audience. The guy running the night was so hunched over, I wondered if he'd ever seen the sky. He must find a lot of pennies.

There were three acts in total—me, a crusty white Rasta called Jah-seph and a buxom called Tina who set about murdering Alanis Morrissette as her gold hoops jangled in a different time zone.

> *I swear I saw her spray perfume up her crotch before she went on. It's like ten thousand twats when all you need is a dick. Yes, it is ironic.*

I played my two songs, but no one gave a shit. One of the yellow trolls at the bar shouted for me to play something they all knew. I said I didn't do covers. He said don't do nothing, as he cackled at death's door.

I wasn't in a rush to go back. I stayed home instead, watched movies, listened to Dice's records, digging for inspiration to help me paint my masterpiece. I wrote countless songs, but nothing was satisfying enough. I hoped that through probability I'd come up with the goods eventually. My passable hit rate was about fifteen to one.

Keep going. And don't worry about the gigs. The live act comes later. Think about those dregs of society sitting alone in the Goose and Granite in years to come, staring mindlessly at that shitty tube in the corner when Jools Holland comes on and introduces you. 'Solitude is the path', etc.

I got really sick. Some fluey type thing that floored me. After a week I was skinny, pale and exhausted. I must've lost a stone and a half in weight. My skin was greasy. I had a huge spot on the top of my cheek that wouldn't go away. It darkened to a dirty purple bruise and ached with infection, my immune system on holiday. I probably should've gone to a doctor but I didn't have one—didn't know where to begin looking for one either. I called in sick to work and bought some fruit and paracetamol for the first time in my life.

Any other ailments you should've seen a doctor about, sir?

I was having my fever dreams again, waking up in cold sweat, muscles rigid from shaking.

What else? Come on, don't be embarrassed.

My gums were red and felt gross and scaly.

You had an infection in your dick and your piss stank like a packet of Frazzles!

I didn't like the start of my sickness coinciding with a letter arriving from New Zealand.

Your mum wrote everything in small capitals. Sick-notes had been an easy racket.

I didn't read it, just hid it under my bed to start what would become quite the collection. My temperature soared and I'd been bed-ridden since.

Just a coincidence?

It was Friday afternoon and I was curled up on the sofa, watching Magnolia and feeling mighty sorry for myself. The door suddenly flew open. Dice bounced in as a storm of frogs rained down on the screen from Hollywood skies—Exodus style.

'Want an adventure? Get your things, man!'

He stopped and looked at me—poorly and smothered under my coverless duvet, asking if I was sick.

'I'm getting better,' I managed.

'That's the spirit,' said Dice.

It was Glastonbury weekend. He could get us in if we got our shit together.

Yes please!

I groaned meekly, said I could barely stand. He moved to the sofa and knelt beside me, swung a rucksack off his back.

Lucky for you he's a doctor.

He pulled a wrap of speed out and insisted I take the medicine. I paused for a second, but in all honesty I felt so rough I'd have let him blow it up my arse if I thought it would help. I dabbed gingerly at the powder and we watched the end of Magnolia again, the storm of reptiles on repeat.

> *We may be through with the past, but the past is not through with us! That speed levelled you out nicely, but imagine what it could do if you got stuck in? It's not gonna stop till you wise up.*

Two hours later we were headed for Glastonbury in Dice's bright yellow Rascal van. He'd bought me some water and a cooked chicken, which I'd devoured before we even got out of the city. The stereo in the van was busted so we sang like obnoxious assholes down the 303.

> *Dice does a mean Bowie. Fucker was so in the zone he didn't see that roundabout coming up though. I thought you were going over! You had to pull into a layby to let out the laughter. Another anecdote. How's about another dab for the chapter?*

I don't know how long we were driving for. We got swallowed by the pagan hills and when we finally pulled into a field outside the festival, the sun was coming up. We'd missed Friday in its entirety! I was starting to feel nauseous from the comedown and whatever remnants of the bug I was still nursing. I ran my fingers over the infected bruise on my face—still there, still tender. Dice's eyes were all over the place, but he was determined to keep going and break in before the day fully arrived. He pointed at some old guys in yellow jackets standing at the entrance of a lane by two cornfields.

We need to sneak past those fuckers.

We sketched up the road away from the attendants, and with a quick look over our shoulders, we jumped over a ditch into the cornfield, started darting through the channels like little Jenny Gump legging it from her dad. The corn was dripping with dew and we were soaking wet immediately. At the other end of the field, we skipped over the gate and ducked through a yard into a cowshed, hopscotching over the dung piles. It smelt like my childhood. I didn't want to let that in.

Me neither. Keep going.

Through the cowshed we swung our way into another yard and saw a track up ahead, punters dragging tents on wheels with crates of booze over their shoulders. We mustered a high-five and dragged our drenched carcasses towards the action, casually merging with the flow of pedestrians and trying to act normal. They were lining up to get onto a minibus. Dice poked the shoulder of a girl in front—his fingers a jittery drum-fill.

147

Where's this bus going?

She looked at Dice like he'd pissed himself, stepping away as she answered.

'Glastonbury. Where d'you think?'

We stopped following and stepped out of the queue, the situation snapping into focus. We were at a pick-up point in the wrong town, still ten miles from the festival! We'd snuck through fields and farmyards like a couple of calamitous burglars for nothing.

My brain was on spin cycle as the dew on my soaked clothes caught the morning breeze and gave me goose-bumps all the way to the bone. Dice started laughing.

'And we left our bags in the van!'

I felt like I was going to throw up.

Better out than in. Dice dragged you back to the van like the gentleman he is, even helped you get changed into some dry clothes, lent you a jumper.

I woke up with the sun beating on the side of the van, roasting me in a yellow oven. I actually felt better than I had in ages, still a little rough, but it wasn't the illness I was nursing, it was more like a midweek hangover—nothing that a cigarette and a can of Coke couldn't cure. I must've sweated or vomited the bug out of me. I could handle a hangover. I actually quite liked them. Good time to reflect.

See? A natural.

Dice wasn't there, but there was a fresh bag of chips and something pissy looking in a bottle by my head. I sat up and opened the van. The country air cleansed my stuffy lungs as I munched on the chips, no clue as to whether it was breakfast, lunch or dinner. We weren't parked where we were last night. I could see the festival for real now, hear muffled basslines from over the brow.

I could see Dice bouncing between cars and campers, thumbs up and headed towards me. He walks like he's got a stone in his shoe. Or one leg shorter than the other?

'Finish them chips! Let's go!' he shouted.

> *There was a fella with a stepladder by the fence. He only had a small window. And brain apparently.*

The chips were cold and stodgy in my dry mouth.

'I need a drink.'

Dice reached past me and grabbed the bottle of piss.

> *Vodka and Red Bull. A Saturday morning pick-me-up.*

I paused for thought. I'd never had spirits before. I'd never had speed either, but I hadn't flinched at the prospect yesterday. The thought of vodka made me nervous for some reason.

I hopped onto the grass, my legs needing a second to steady themselves, then I checked my complexion in the wing mirror. The crimson carbuncle on my cheek was still very much there—ugly fucking thing.

'Pass me that vodka.'

Fuelled and primed. Let's go find Pea Brain and his master plan. It was more of a stack of beer-crates than a stepladder, but hey, no drama, you first. Dice came flailing down on top of you like Wile E. Coyote, brushed himself off and told you he was immortal. I for one believed him.

We were in! Dodging through a web of guy ropes, I had no idea what time it was or where we were going, hadn't thought about the fact we didn't have a tent or anything resembling a camping trip. I didn't even know who was playing that year, but I was so stoked to be there. Glastonbury had always been on my hit list. I'd taped some clips off the telly in New Zealand when I was younger, pining for England. That was the year Blur and Oasis headlined. I wore the video out devouring inspiration from it, picturing myself on that main stage many times.

Showing them how it's done.

We reached a patch of woods. There were drapes and glitter balls hanging from the canopies, booming dub bass rumbled in the trees from a pink and silver bullet, knees swinging, rainbow dreadlocks, khaki face paint. It wasn't what I came to see but Dice started to bob about, told me to skin up while he got us some water.

He skipped off towards an ice-cream van while I rolled. When he came back he shook my hand, stroking a pill into my palm. It had a Superman logo on it. Dice smiled and threw his arms out straight in front of him, started miming flight.

'Is it a bird? Is it a plane?'

He asked me if I'd done ecstasy before. I hadn't. I didn't really know what it was. I thought it was for nightclubbing, which I couldn't stand. Not that I'd ever done that either. Just the thought of the music they played put me off. Too repetitive. Nothing resembling a narrative I could get my teeth into.

Stop overcomplicating everything. There's beauty in simplicity too. Get that pill down your neck.

I swallowed the tablet, washed it thirstily down with a bottle of water. Dice reckoned it'd take about half an hour to start working. I didn't want to be under those trees when I came up.

Suit yourself.

I wanted to get into the open for a bit, go stand in front of that main stage and tick a box off in my mind. Dice couldn't care less.

'Whatever man. You'll be back once Superman arrives.'

How's that for simple?

I could see the back of the pyramid stage, a beacon from my dreams. I set off, changing directions when I needed to, but keeping my eyes fixed on the destination at all times, my Converse kneading sticky mud, the pace pumping the blood and the pill around my veins. I got to the field and made a beeline for the mixing desk in the middle. I didn't know who was on. Didn't care. I just wanted to take the sight in, tattoo the reality onto the fantasy.

The pyramid field slopes down to the stage. There must've been ten thousand people spread out on picnic blankets at the top half, gradually merging into another ten thousand stood in loosely woven packs, dancing in the sunshine. Superman was on his way. Fuzzy hands were massaging the organ in my skull. My intestines tingled and my thin pins grew weightless as I tripped along through the bodies, Clark Kent's fingertips gripping my jumper, about to rip it open.

There's a reason they call it ecstasy.

At the mixing desk I turned to the stage, a wonderous miracle. I remembered seeing the *Almond Blossom* in Amsterdam and felt a twinge of anxiety, hoped the great pyramid wouldn't awaken any unwelcome home truths in me. It didn't. It couldn't. Anxiety had no place in the universe I'd just arrived in. I was a bona fide Man of Steel!

The band started a song I recognised. It was Let's Stay Together from Pulp Fiction. Fucking Al Green was a hundred yards away singing Let's Stay Together! I couldn't help but swing my rubbery legs, nod my dough-ball head on a slinky neck, singing at the top of my lungs. When suddenly...

'William?'

She remembered your name.

She emerged from the crowd like an air bubble from the deep—mud-brown hair and fearless hazel eyes.

What an extraordinary buzz kill!

'Oh my god! William!'
She gathered me up in her blissful arms. My gurning jaw dropped and I felt heaven upon me.
'Jess!'

Why some people break up? Then turn around and make up?

I was speechless, high as a kite and overwhelmed to the brink of hallucination. It all happened so fast. Jess was with a hoard of friends that swept behind her—merry on the pop no doubt and on some kind of group mission to get from one place to another in the bustling festival.

Well, first of all, why would you want to leave when Al Green is on?

Her group of friends were too pissed to engage in what had just happened, couldn't have had a clue about the significance. They tugged noisily at Jess's arm, marching as a pack trying to steal her away. She wriggled free, facing me down with a great big smile. I was suddenly thinking about the bruise on my face, the slack in my pale jaw.

She could see her friends disappearing into the abyss of the crowd—lost for certain if she didn't go. I couldn't move my feet. She looked right at me again. The detail of my ill being must've snapped her into focus. Her wide smile straightened off and faded, buoyancy in her step coming to rest, eyes narrowing, puzzled by the specimen in front of her. I felt revolting—an object of pity consumed with disappointment in itself.

To whose standards?

Jess's friends were shouting for her. She looked worried, serious. Fucking hell, I wished I could read her mind. She reached into her satchel and pulled out a lipstick, rolled up my sleeve and started scrawling on my arm. Then she hugged me and whispered.

'Make it happen.'

Is that really what she said?

And with that she disappeared between the bodies. I was rooted in the mud as their heads bobbed away, the ecstasy making everything melt together like watercolour.

I willed the gravity back into my soupy legs and gave chase, but she was lost. I was lost. Now I wished I really was Superman. I wanted to fly around the earth backwards, rewind the world an hour and say no to Dice! I wanted to gather Jess in my arms and take her flying over the metropolis. To stand a chance of finding her, I needed to get the drugs out of my system. On whatever walkway I'd found myself on, I stopped and stuck my fingers down my throat—bile and chips from the well in my belly.

A moment of madness, William. I'll allow it for circumstance.

I walked the festival for a couple of hours like a feather in a wind tunnel, but as I finally started coming down, I realised what it was I had to do.

It was dark when I eventually found the van. It was locked and Dice had the keys. Fuck knows where he was.

Keeping it real somewhere I imagine.

With the last of my last fumes, I dragged myself onto the roof, happy to find room and board beneath the stars, with the festival in my ears like a neighbour's garden party. I was out like a light.

I woke up to the sound of Dice coughing his lungs up, fumbling with the van keys. I was freezing but at least the ecstasy had gone. For the first time in an age, something other than a cigarette had entered my mind on waking.

Realising you weren't thinking about cigarettes is the same as thinking about cigarettes, dummy.

I slid off the roof, startling Dice who just laughed as he unlocked the van, his face like a Francis Bacon. He mumbled incoherently, climbed into the driver's seat

and passed out on the steering wheel. He looked dead.
I looked away.

Don't worry. He's still breathing.

I jumped into the back, grabbing all the clothing I could
to wrap myself up in. Physically I was drained, but
mentally I'd found a life raft.

Says you.

Alone you stand with nobody near, when a trembling,
distant voice unclear, startles your sleeping ears to hear,
that somebody thinks they really found you.

They're just words.

As the temperature rose in the yellow oven, I had one
thing on my mind—glossy and sharp in a monochrome
vision. Jess and the phone number scrawled in lipstick
up my arm.

157

10 Got to Keep the DEVIL Down in the HOLE

Soapy rubber gloves shifted the willy to the side and began scrubbing a flannel on the leathery scrotum hanging loose like an old string bag.

'Looks a bit sore down here Patrick,' said Angela—kind gemstone eyes and loose burgundy ponytail.

Patrick said nothing. He was standing stark naked on a towel, ninety-year-old skin mottled with patches of wizardy hair, frail hands gripping a lavender sink for stability. Angela asked me to carry on washing his back, bum and legs while she went for some Fucidin. She handed me some rubber gloves from her nurse's tabard and left the room.

'Just gonna carry on giving you a wash Patrick, alright? Then we can get you dressed and back to the snooker,' I said.

He nodded like the gentleman he was and murmured something I couldn't quite make out.

'What's that, mate?' my slippery hands soaping the flannel to wash him as he gently forced the words from his denture-less mouth. He whispered that she was an angel that one.

'Who? Angela?' I asked. 'The clue's in the name, Patrick!'

His short laugh was tired but most definitely real.

Patrick had Parkinson's, mild dementia and a crippling hernia. That he was stood at the sink in his room was something of a miracle. He'd found a lease of life lately because the torment of the dreaded hoist was too much—lowering him in and out of the bath like livestock. He was putting every scrap of energy into saving himself from the ordeal, devoting his existence to mustering strength enough to stand for a hand wash in the morning, even if it meant being stuck in the bucket chair for the rest of the day. The snooker was on at the moment, which made it bearable. It took him fifteen minutes to tell me that, but even if it hadn't, I could've talked to Patrick for hours.

Caring for the elderly is like time travel—a window into the future that can only be imagined. I often wondered what stories I'd be telling as an old man, but I never thought of them being told from inside a home. In terms of character though, I'd settle for being anything remotely close to as dignified as Patrick.

...

The supermarket had sacked me when I didn't come in after my bender at Glastonbury. I'd needed more than a couple of days for my rehabilitation and I had the sacking coming anyway. It wasn't like I was an indispensable member of the team. I gave up drinking and cut out the fags, didn't want to see drugs of any kind. Dice had done his usual and disappeared—for months this time—which made it all pretty easy.

I replaced the time it took to smoke a cigarette with an orderly task—alphabetise the records, read a book, make a piece of cheese on toast, run around the block. I tidied the flat, finally got someone round to unblock the stagnant sink, and bought a rug for my floor. It really tied the room together, man.

Instead of drinking in the evening, I set about learning a new song from Dice's collection every night, furthering my education and adding to my repertoire. I lived on bananas and pasta, gaining much-needed weight, regenerating my sugary insides and kicking my immune system back into play. The bruise on my face was gone by the time I started my new job.

...

I'd applied for the only one I didn't need qualifications for, a care assistant for the elderly mentally ill—an EMI unit. The irony that 'EMI' was also one of the biggest record labels wasn't lost on me. It was as close as I was going to get. Dice was never around. I was starting to think his talk of the record industry was all bullshit. I'd given up on trying to write songs for now. Nothing felt original now that my tastes had been expanded.

Music became a useful hobby while I put my health first. I was in a good place though—happy at work and Jess back in my life, albeit at the end of a telephone.

Yawn.

I was nervous the first time we spoke. I didn't know what questions she'd ask or how she'd think of me. She'd tried to be my friend after what happened all those years ago, but I was elsewhere, didn't want to see anyone. And when we moved to New Zealand I didn't keep in touch.

Having been hoping she wouldn't want to talk about the past, when it didn't come up at all, it was actually kind of weird.

You made it weird.

All she wanted to talk about was her life at university in Bath, and it made her sound really young. Not in her voice necessarily, but in the way she spoke. It was different to how I'd imagined it would be. Different to how I wanted it to be. It was all quite unexpected.

What do you mean?

It was like nothing had changed for her except the size of her school. Like she was still a kid, whereas I was a globe-trotting, car-driving, workin' man? I don't know. Listening indifferently to the canteen politics, I felt like she was my little sister or something.

Whoa, whoa, whoa! Be very careful what seeds you plant my incestuous friend. You may have lived in Cornwall but you weren't born there. Back away from that thought and remember the time you saw her nipples accidently.

I was far less disappointed than I thought I'd be though.

Oh my god, there's work to be done here.

She wanted to know about New Zealand, imagining it as some mystical paradise. I fed her vision, didn't really want to go into details. I told her I was in London to become a musician and that things were slow but moving in the right direction. She sounded impressed. I lied about the ecstasy. I told her that when she saw me at Glastonbury I'd been sick with a virus and had to get taken home, that I was gutted she saw me that way, but that I was all better now.

'It was your smile I recognised,' she said sweetly.

And why were you smiling, Clark Kent?

She had a boyfriend. It was some guy she had lectures with—Ben from business studies. I was happy for her, like a big brother would be.

Gross.

She was going away with her family for the summer but would be back in September, would love to meet up, would love me to meet Ben.

She has to say that though.

'Sure thing.'

Smooth.

It would be a couple of months until we saw each other. I was focused on work, focused on something other than my dreams. Weeks rolled by. I hadn't touched a drink or a smoke, though I still thought about it a lot.

Cleaning up will only disarm you. It'd be like taking your fists to a gun fight. Don't do it.

'How old are you?' asked Angela in the staffroom at work, midsummer, supping a rusty builder's tea.
'Eighteen.'
'Don't be daft!'
She said I was far too mature to be eighteen. It took guts to take the job on at my age, she said. It was heavy and grotty. She said she knew blokes twice my age that couldn't hack it. That wiping old arse and washing old bollocks was too much for them to handle, but that I just got on with it with a big smile on my face.
'Scrubbing nuts does *not* put a smile on my face, thank you, Angela.'

Her laugh was at least ten decibels louder than anyone else's and entirely infectious. She was ace—a funny and forward no-nonsense northerner with courageous blue December eyes. She had a wicked sense of humour and I looked forward to work because of her, learnt much about bedside manner, patience and kindness.

'How old are you?' I asked, returning from the sidetrack.

She teased me and said I was showing my age now. It wasn't polite to ask that of a lady.

'Hang on—Lady?' I said in uproar. 'Would a lady fart quite so blatantly as you do?'

She gasped, blushing at the memory.

We'd been getting Joan Butterly ready for the day last week. She was a super sweet lady in her eighties who was very much embarrassed about not being able to care for herself anymore. Joan accidently farted when we lifted her from her wheelchair and, to deflect the shame, Angela selflessly squeezed one out and Joan was in hysterics. So was I. So was Angela. She went bright red and palmed her face.

Back in the staffroom, I asked cheekily again.

'So how old are you? Or do you want me to start holding the doors? Put my coat over the puddles and pick up the cheque?'

'You taking me on a date?' she grinned. 'How old do you think I am?'

I went with my instinct, which said twenty-two.

'Don't I just love you?!' she laughed and told me she was twenty-eight.

'Bollocks!' I decried. 'Now who's being daft?'

She smothered her smile into a crisp sandwich.

'How old is Jess?' she asked sideways. 'Is that your friend's name?'

She hadn't been on my mind in a while. I brushed away a small pang of guilt that I wasn't making more effort with Jess, but the intensity of the job and staying healthy felt like fair distraction.

...

St Mary's nursing home was dank and run down, managed by a bat-shit crazy toff called Elizabeth and her lapdog husband. Apart from him and the chef, I was the only male working there when I started—probably why I got the job. It wasn't physically exhausting, but it was hard not to get emotionally sucked in even if you only had one compassionate bone in your body. It was shitty pay for what it took from you and, as such, it seemed the only people able to withstand longevity in the job lacked empathy and prospects. Most of the nurses were blunt and self-obsessed, gossiping across the residents under the assumption that their mental state meant they didn't understand. A sensitive side made the job so much harder, dragged you down in the sadness of it all. I'd seen a number of worthy staff come and go already, unable to balance the emotional draining with the low income. Not Angela though. She made it her mission to be a beacon of hope. I was inspired to follow suit and we became each other's buoyancy.

Between meals, toilet runs and bath times was where the treasure from the toil lay. It was a chance to sit and speak to the residents while writing up the changeover notes. Some were more capable of chat than others and some straight up didn't want to. I got the fright of my life when I politely asked Gwen if I could sit with her for a while.

'Why would I want to sit with you, you cunt?'

She looked like an Edvard Munch painting! How did you think it would go? An hour before you'd been fishing her own poo out of her mouth with your fingers, hadn't you? Hardly a sweet old grandma.

There were so many stories to uncover, histories deteriorating in a prison of sickly wallpaper and tasteless liquid dinners. Patrick's were my favourite. He'd been an artist, married a Belgian seamstress after the war and travelled around Africa pioneering a water pump powered by a children's roundabout. Listening to his stories was like meditation. Sometimes I'd stay after my shift to watch sport with him but that was causing issues with the pricks on night duty. They'd insist he got put to bed even if I offered to do it myself later. I could only argue so much. I couldn't afford to lose my job.

Aren't you the saint?

I was all in all grounded.

Knock, knock.

Dice came home late one night. It was the first time I'd seen him in months—since Glastonbury in fact. He'd shaved his head, lost weight. He looked like a stray Siamese cat—much more triangular without the curtains. He looked pissed off that I'd made the place my own. He didn't say anything, just stood in the living room and perused with a stain of annoyance I hadn't seen before, his usual bounce absent.

You got his rent? It has to be cash.

I apologised because I didn't have any cash. I'd opened a bank account and would have to get it tomorrow. He mumbled and bit his fingernails, spat them at the beer-crate coffee table, missing the empty ashtray. Then he said he had to put my rent up and fixed an awkward icy gaze.

You've had it sweet, mate.

He scanned around again, flexing his jaw.
  'Where's the phone?'
  I'd moved it so I could sit by the window and talk in the chair.
  'You been using the phone? You have to pay for that. And bills. I'm never here so you pay the bills too.'
  With no defence all I could do was try and soften the tone.
  'Is everything alright?'

That stare again.

He helped you, now you help him.

I wanted him to leave.

'I can come and find you tomorrow after work. Where you gonna be?' I offered.

His shorter leg juddered at full stretch as he sussed me out.

'Something's come up,' he snapped. 'I'm staying here for a couple of nights. Sort me out tomorrow.'

And with that he went to the kitchen, started pulling out drawers like he was looking for something, opening cupboards and huffing at everything like it was too much to process. I didn't stick around. I found puzzled quiet in my curtain-less room, the city's sparkle muted by a dull fog.

It all seemed fair enough.

After work the next day, I came home to find Dice restless in the living room like he'd been standing there waiting the whole time. I gave him his money—a tough handover. I wondered where the guy I'd met six months ago was. He barely said goodbye, just bolted out of my life for another welcome spell of peace.

...

'Half a Coke and a pint of Guinness please,' I ordered.

The Coke was for me, the Guinness for Angela. The barman put the drinks down, having made the wrong assumption about whose was whose. Angela pushed the Coke over to me and took her Guinness.

'I think not!'

The pub quiz was about to start. Angela had meant to be there with another friend but they'd bailed last minute. It was a rare night she'd found a babysitter for her son, Archie, so she called me up and asked if I wanted to come so she didn't miss the opportunity.

She'd arrived late, apologising for Archie having been unsettled. He was only four. I'd met him a few times when she brought him in to collect her payslip. He had bright orange curls and blue-rimmed glasses that made his eyes sing.

'Hey, little man. What do you want to be when you grow up?' I'd asked

'A helicopter driver.'

'Yeah? How come?'

'Coz you only have to use one hand.'

Needless to say, I loved this kid.

I hadn't recognised Angela outside of work. She was rocking a tie-dye top under a dark denim jacket, black skinny jeans and DC skate shoes well worn in. She must've been a grunger in her day. I'd never seen her with her hair down, brushing dyed scarlet across her shoulders. There was no way she was twenty-eight.

Angela asked if I didn't drink. I took a moment.

'Not really. You go ahead though.'

She said she had every intention of doing so, sipping at the froth, which did look delicious. This was a rare treat for her and she was taking full advantage.

I don't know how to describe the feeling that came over me then. My head felt like a helium balloon, tethered to sturdy shoulders. All I could see was what was in front of me. The people and pub, living in the now. My words came out of nowhere.

'My dad was an alcoholic.'

I couldn't believe what I'd said. I was sure she'd spit her drink out, fire questions at me, churn up the past, view me as a complicated victim that needed therapy instead of friendship.

'Mine was too,' she said casually. 'Arsehole.'

And that was that. I landed safely, grinning ear to ear as the quiz started.

'Which singer-songwriter has composed such songs as Jockey Full of Bourbon, Gin Soaked Boy and The Piano Has Been Drinking?'

Angela shrieked, prodding me in excitement. 'You must know that?' she said.

'Clearly I'm a fraud!'

'You never heard Tom Waits?'

I was ashamed to say I hadn't. 'W' was at the end of Dice's records and I was still only on 'S' for Spooky Tooth. Angela ribbed me for showing my age again.

We gave up on the quiz halfway through, far more entertained making light of each other's generation. I stayed on the Coke all night.

Yawn. Goodness me.

Waiting at the bus stop Angela kissed my cheek, grateful for the opportunity to wind down. She was tipsy and didn't want to leave. I was stone cold sober, but I felt the same. She was staring at me with those two gemstones, looking like she was gonna lean in and kiss me again.

'What am I doing?' she said, as if catching herself, placing her hands on flushing cheeks.

She said I should be hanging around with my other friends. People my own age. I ignored the fact I had no other friends and joked she was being an ageist Manc. She was quick to correct me.

'Actually, I was born in Macclesfield.'

Neither of us knew what to do next. Taxis caught left-over puddles and upper decks floated above slick streets. To break the silence, she asked me if I was in work on Friday. I suddenly remembered something.

'Oh shit!'

Here we go.

I'd swapped my shifts coz I was meant to be visiting Jess in Bath this weekend.

Unlucky!

Angela hailed her bus as it came round the corner. She thanked me again and gave me a hug.

No kisses this time.

I waved her off as she floated down the street.

Jess's friends are a bunch of fucking drips, aren't they?
Actually, scratch that—privileged, boring, stuck-up,
trust-fund, udder-sucking cunts. Alright, so you nailed
your paper on 'Who gives a fuck?' for your degree
in 'Suck my balls'! And oh wow, you did what every
other student that's ever lived did and set off the fire
extinguishers? My hero! What did Jess see in them?
So immature. And Ben? Boat-shoes Ben from busi-
ness reckoned he was a musician, playing Wish You
Were Here like he'd just written it himself. Old news
I'm afraid, put your collar down and stay in your lane.
All the charisma of a boiled egg. Should've grabbed the
guitar off him sooner. Smug prick. Scratch that—smug,
condescending, self-righteous, royal rectum, sipping on
a bottle of piss with his jealous eye on Jess the whole
time. William, I told you not to disarm yourself. Your
clarity was costing you. Jess was sweet as ever with a
body to die for but you couldn't get close. Congratula-
tions on your sobriety but enough was enough, time to
unleash the beast. I mean—the conqueror.

I was an alien trapped among earthlings that couldn't
understand me. They appeared to be partaking in some
kind of ritual where they drink of a potion that comes
in bottles and are then able to find humour in things
that aren't funny. Perhaps if I drink of that same potion,
I could find a way to communicate?

If you can't beat them…

The next time a tray of shots came round, I said fuck it and joined in. I hated the taste of sambuca but I followed with familiarity—beer, wine and cigarettes. I soon caught up.

'Giz a turn on the guitar.'

> *Ladies and Gentlemen, raise the roof to your entertainment for the evening. That showed them. Johnny Jukebox. If you didn't know the song they threw at you, you only had to hear it once. They'd never seen anything like that. Never met anyone like you. An old friend of Jess's—the quiet, mysterious Kiwi—suddenly the life and soul. Jess was saying, I told you so! I told you so! Her best friend Molly was swooning. Drunk, yes, but you show your true feelings when you're drunk, eh, Jake da Muss? Cook da man some fucken' iggs!!*

The room was mine—the audience in the palm of my hand.

> *Ben's jealousy made him drink more to keep up, but there was no way back for him. He stodged out like Droopy, dead-weight on the sofa, annoyingly not letting go of his prize—Jess perched on his knee. Jess was jealous too—of you and Molly flinging strawpedos down your throats, playing Oasis B-sides, ripping through the whole of Hotel California, solo and all. One by one the students caved in and went to bed. Molly kissed you goodnight. Jess raised the ante and ran her fingers through your hair, out of Ben's line of sight, but not from*

Molly's. Oh no. She wanted her to know you weren't there for the taking. Oh yes.

I polished off a glass of someone else's wine and crashed out on the sofa, the last man standing at the so-called party. Face squashed into the armrest, I could feel my heart pumping double time as I pondered my triumph.

You're welcome.

I was a grown-up with a degree in life under my belt. The entrance music was blaring and I was stepping into the ring. It'd been useful to go teetotal, educate myself and get clean, but I was healthy now, bursting with ideas that'd been festering. Having a drink to loosen up brought my dreams back out of the closet, ten-fold. I told myself it would be useful for Dutch courage at open mics at the very least. I wasn't an addict. I wasn't my dad. I needed to get back out playing.

Exactly.

On the train home to London, I stared happily out of the window, yawning and gobbling up the candyfloss clouds, autumn's treasures on the breeze.

Remember how Jess squeezed you at the train station? Told me everything I needed to know. How about you?

I was returning to London with my dream of becoming a superstar back on the table—a feast fit for a king.

Those record labels won't know what's hit them.

There was a girl with Down's syndrome sat opposite with her mum. She had a bright red apple in one hand and a giant bag of crisps in the other. She wasn't interested in the apple but, instead of putting it down to eat the crisps, she was dipping her mouth into the bag and snuffling them out one at a time. Her mum was reading a book called Families and How to Survive Them. I caught eye contact with the girl—golden pigtails and checked blue dress. We shared a moment and I leant over.

'Hey, look,' I said softly, pointing at the apple—nature's ruby.

Her mum looked up as I took the fruit from the girl's hand and placed it in front of her, pointing at her freed fingers, gesturing that she could now eat the snacks with ease.

'Now you can get more!' I smiled.

The girl looked at me for a beat, then picked the apple back up and sank her front teeth in. She took a huge crunch out and chewed it up gleefully. Her mum smiled at me. I shrugged and reciprocated, shuffled in my seat ready for a power nap—closing my eyes, pursuing the dreams and feeling immortal.

You got enough change to get some fags?

Home. 124 Daubeney Tower. In the eight months I'd lived there, I realised I hadn't gotten to know a single person from the other flats. Plenty of strangers passed by, but I preferred my imagination to the reality. I'd make up all kinds of shit about their lives.

Sky-high and out of the lift, I waved my fob at the sensor and strutted down the corridor, my footsteps squeaking like a screw from Scum's borstal. As I pushed on through the front door, I could hear music coming from the living room. It was eighties era Dylan—maybe Knocked Out Loaded? Dice's sheepskin bomber jacket was hanging on the coat hook. I followed the din.

He was sat in my seat with a can of special brew. He looked much better than last time I saw him, displaying that familiar Cheshire grin as he offered me a can as a peace offering.

'Hey, man. Sorry for being an asshole,' he said. 'Some shit went down, but we're all good now.'

I took the drink—not much twisting of the arm occurring—as Dice sparked a Camberwell carrot. He was moving back in. Was ready to help me pursue my dreams again.

It wasn't Knocked Out Loaded, it was Infidels.

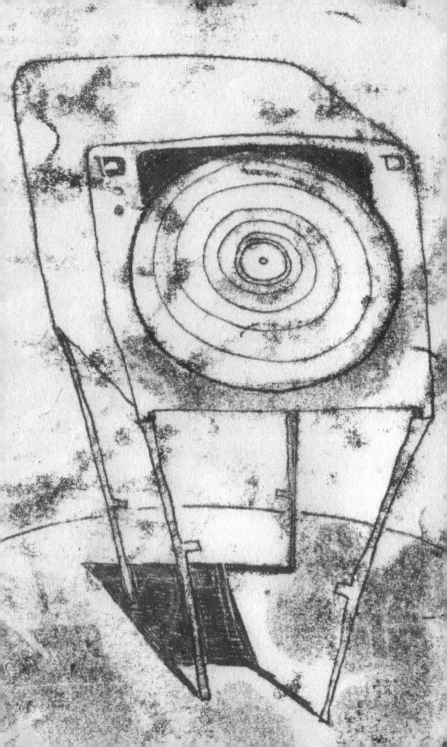

11 Do What i say
and i'll make you okay,
Drive them Away

Crank it up!

I hit play on the portable stereo. The girl behind reception looked like she was merely humouring me. I was confident that would change when she heard my demos though.

Dice was mooching about in the foyer, voicing his approval while looking at the gold discs framed all over the walls—Led Zeppelin, The Rolling Stones, Tom Waits.

Atlantic Records will do nicely, thanks.

The girl didn't seem impressed by track one, but that was fine. I knew there were another nineteen tracks on this CD alone. And I had another thirty on two more CDs in my bag. If she didn't dig *this* song, I could skip to another for as long as it took until her interest was inevitably piqued. Then she'd welcome me in, past reception, take me straight to the top floor to interrupt the MD and demand she get credit for discovering me. She hadn't budged or said anything yet though.

She wasn't paying the right kind of attention.

She wasn't paying the right kind of attention.

'Let me skip to the next one. You'll like the next one.'
I hoped.

She said, no thanks, it wasn't what they were looking for.

'There's loads more. All different.'

She said it wasn't the right vibe. She could tell.

How could she tell without listening to it all?

'How can you tell without listening to it all?'

She was typing on a computer, didn't make eye contact. I couldn't decipher a colour from the cyan reflection of the monitor. I ignored her wishes and let the CD roll to the next track, turned it up a little. I was reaching for an F in my best Tom Waits voice, circa Closing Time. I was back on the fags but not to the level that would give me the Blue Valentine husk I wanted.

She's not concentrating.

'You're not concentrating.'

She asked me sternly to turn it off, said I could leave a CD behind and she'd pass it on.

I sighed, switching the music off. How could anyone make a judgement without hearing the whole story? It made no sense to me.

How could anyone make a judgement without hearing the whole story? It made no sense to me.

This was the fifth record label we'd come to and the first where we'd got to play anything at all. The others had ushered us out immediately, telling us we could leave a CD behind. I left copies with all of them—over fifty songs made under the name William The Conqueror.

A smart, handsome man with chocolate eyes and a cashmere sweater had come in across the lobby and folded his arms behind reception, observing the scene and hiding a smirk behind flared nostrils.

Maybe this guy can help?

Dice could sense it was time for some managerial intervention and hobbled over from the discs, started rambling about what a great talent I was, that he'd been in the industry for ten years and had never seen anything like me. One half of me blushed while the other played peacock.

'It's very straightforward,' said Dice to the two of them. 'We're looking for a development deal. We need support from a label like yourselves to put the band together and find us an agent. Say, a hundred grand for the record and some tour budget, and you guys cover the legal fees. Can you call someone down from A&R please?'

The girl didn't pick up the phone, but her eyes widened and she spoke without looking.

'There's no one around this time of year. Everyone's either out or they've gone home for Christmas.'

'It's the beginning of December!' Dice implored, dissatisfied. 'You telling me the record industry goes to sleep at the beginning of December?'

She looked at her colleague, who raised his svelte brow and spoke up. He was cool, calm and confident.

'If you've been in the industry for ten years then you should know, shouldn't you?' he said in an unexpected, buttery French accent.

'I'm from A&R. Can I have a look at the CDs?'

I handed them over and he studied the great long list of song titles on the back. Flipping to the front, the covers were all the same—just the name in hard black pencil. A total *Black Rider* rip-off.

'William The Conqueror? Good name. You have any gigs coming up?' he asked.

'I've been doing open mics.'

He seemed unimpressed. 'I could do that myself,' he said.

I told him that live comes later.

So you were listening!

He let out a short laugh, the way a teacher does when a kid he likes says something naive. Then he dispensed a lesson he thought we needed.

'Actually, it all has to come together at the same time. The song is one element, but if you want it to work, there's all these other elements too. Playing live is one of them. A very important one. You should be gigging, getting a name for yourself, being part of a scene, learning your trade. And that's just the beginning! Get a label and there are even *more* things to think about. And they *all* need to work together if you want it to work. Think of it like you're a plate spinner.'

His Rolex wrists shook as he moved his arms around, spinning metaphorical plates one by one, naming them as he went.

'*Live* performance. You need an *agent*. *Merchandise*. You need a *publisher*. A *publicist*. An *image. Fan base*. All going at the same time.'

He stepped away from the invisible plates, admiring the spectacle for a moment before concluding.

'No one cares about the guy who only has one plate.'

Dice chimed in.

'They would if the plate was the size of a roundabout,' he said, pretending to heave and wrench a tree-sized pole from side to side.

Good point.

'And anyway –' Dice stopped the miming, thank god. 'How can we get all that going if we don't have some money to do it?' he reasoned. 'It's the chicken and the egg.'

'How is it the chicken and the egg?' said the girl, annoyed that we were still there.

Dice huffed. 'It's what came first, isn't it? Chicken or egg? We can't get the gigs without the agent and we can't get the agent without the deal.'

'That's a catch-twenty-two,' said the man, getting smoother by the minute. 'No chickens. No eggs.'

The girl sniggered.

Look at these dummies. What did they know? How could they understand an artist as deep and as interesting as you? Probably from wealthy, wholesome families with endless chapters of privilege buoying them up. Probably never known bad luck or drama. Probably headed to the broom cupboard for a Christmas frisson once we're gone! Forget them.

'What sort of music are you looking for?' I asked, frustrated.

'What sort of music are you looking for?' came the rebuttal.

Dice jumped in.

'The kind that'll still be around in fifty years' time!'

The man turned his eyes first, then his head, to Dice. 'And who are you?'

'I'm his manager. Who are you?'

He curled the corners of his mouth down, looked like De Niro in Sleepers. 'My name's Duncan.'

Duncan The Forgettable.

'Can I take these?'

Duncan's watch rattled again as he brandished the demos.

What a U-turn! I take it back, Duncan. Tu es magnifique!

'Of course! Absolutely!' I said excitedly.

Duncan put the CDs on the counter and produced a marker pen from the desk, frowned at Dice like a disappointed parent.

'You might want to write your contact down somewhere then.'

What a schoolboy error. We hadn't put the contacts on any of the other CDs we'd handed out. What a fucking waste of a day that was! Oh well, it didn't dull the excitement.

As Dice hurried to write the contacts down, Duncan gave nothing away, cards kept close to his cashmere chest.

'You've certainly written a lot of songs,' he finally offered.

'Over three hundred,' I said proudly.

'Well,' said Duncan, curling his mouth again. 'All it takes is one.'

> *You owe Dice big time. Let's celebrate with some ginger wine and a fat one. Then sit back and wait for the phone call. You've as good as made it now.*

The bosses at St Mary's had split mine and Angela's shifts up. They cited some bullshit about team building, but I know they did it out of spite. Our friendship and good intentions made them look like the arseholes they were.

It was definitely more depressing without a like-minded buddy to share the time with. I thought long and hard about my imminent career change to keep me skipping.

I've been thinking about that whole plate-spinning analysis—networking, irons in the fire and what not. Basically, it's bollocks. A total cliché. Dice is right about focusing solely on the songs. It's the centrepiece they need but don't have. I've been trying to tell you that for years—one giant, go-fuck-yourself plate sawing the impenetrable forest to pieces! It's going to take a new kind of devotion from you, but if there's one thing you can definitely do, it's bury your head! Gimme fifty, then get in the sand. Let the label figure out all the other bullshit—with their doilies and their little piddly saucers. They'll see.

At work one night, the snooker had been switched off and Patrick's bucket chair was no longer in front of the telly. I'd nipped out for a fag and the night staff must've seen me leave and pounced. Lazy pricks. The sooner they got the residents to bed, the sooner they could sit on their fat arses and slag the day staff off. I'd stayed on late with Patrick enough times to know that they were all a bunch of shit stirrers.

I ran to Patrick's room. He wasn't there, which meant they were taking him to the bathroom and the dreaded hoist. I found them wheeling his bucket chair through the door.

'Not tonight!' I shouted. 'We're watching the snooker.' Dee the night manager instructed the others to continue while she dealt with me. She had a face like a bulldog and a greasy ponytail stretched back hard in vain, failing to smooth the jowls of a double-divorcee. There was also Stan—the new guy with the dragon tattooed on his face—and Carol—the lady with the face of an actual dragon. Dee blocked my way, telling me Patrick was fast asleep when they went in.

'I was gonna wake him. You know snooker, it goes on. But it's the final!'

I'd learnt to take Dee on gently. The minute you showed signs of defiance, the threats of being sacked would start—she was friends with the bat-shit owners.

'Why aren't you washing him in his room at least?' I said, masking the shaking of my head, the gritting of my teeth. Dee said he needed a bath.

'At ten o'clock at night? Give him a hand wash. Don't put him in the hoist. He hates it.'

She told me not to tell her how to do her job.

I was trying to be diplomatic but there was no reason to her reasons. Stan and Carol were lining up the hoist above Patrick. He was awake now, but he didn't have the energy to show his objections. I tried pleading again with Dee.

'On balance we've come to a good place, right? You let it slide sometimes, I let it slide sometimes, he gets tired, he needs his rest—I understand. But it's the fucking final!'

She told me to watch my mouth and, no, she had too much to do—notes to write and other menial shite she could do perched on her arse.

I offered to stay on. I could do her notes. Patrick was being undressed—breadstick arms raised up by the pull of clumsy Carol tugging his jumper over his head. I shouted at her to stop. Dee didn't budge her concrete stare from me and barked backwards.

'Carry on, Carol!'

Then she brought her voice down to let me know she meant business. 'You don't tell your superiors what to do.'

Superior in job description only, you fucking old cunt.

'Superior in job description only, you fucking old cunt.'

Get on!

Dee fired me on the spot. She said if I left now she wouldn't make a big deal of it to the managers and press bullshit charges. I told myself I didn't give a shit about the job. Duncan had my demos and it was only a matter of time before being up to my ass in cash.

Uh huh.

I wanted to apologise and say goodbye to Patrick though.

Has being soft ever gotten you anywhere?

As they wrenched the levers of the hoist, he swung stark naked and humiliated, the sound of boiling water on full blast echoing off the tiles like deep white noise.

'Patrick, mate. Looks like I lost this one.'

I told him I'd tape the rest of the snooker and bring it in for him to watch tomorrow. Dee took over from Stan, whose Millwall fingers held my arms all the way to the door.

I found a phone box and called home, asked Dice to record the rest of the snooker. He could tape over Lock, Stock and Two Smoking Barrels—that film only needed one viewing. I got home and told him what had happened.

'Nazis man, the lot of 'em.'

Which one of us said that?

We toasted Patrick and watched Stephen Hendry lift the trophy for the umpteenth time.

A friend in need's a friend indeed. A friend with weed is better.

The next morning I took the video to St Mary's.

It wasn't unusual to see an ambulance outside, but this one caught my eye. It seemed familiar. The blue lights spun but no sirens sounded, the doors like an open fridge awaiting leftovers. As I came through into reception, a wet-eyed Angela opened her arms and embraced me.

'What's going on?' I asked.

Patrick had died in his sleep.

'At least he died peacefully,' said Angela.

I knew that wasn't the case. A red mist came over me. Angela let go and realised I wasn't in my uniform.

'What happened? You piss yourself?'

Well that's inappropriate actually. This is no time for jokes, Angela.

I could see Dee talking to the doctor with her files of precious fucking notes, wrapping up another sad tale with empty platitudes—just another day on the job. I moved Angela aside and headed for Dee. She didn't see me coming. I grabbed her files and threw them down the corridor, channelling the venom of an idiot wind.

'No one will be at your side when you die, Dee.'

> *And no song ever sung. Farewell to that bullshit. You didn't need the work anymore. It was better that you got sacked, then you could stay in and wait by the phone. Let's get shit-faced first. Been a while since you tugged on oblivion's collar.*

With no job I was stuck indoors at a loose end most of the time.

> *Or stoned?*

I was watching the pennies and living on fifty-pence pasta, but somehow I always had money for cigarettes, beer and weed. Being stoned ate up the hours of boredom with its time-lapse qualities for sure. And generally it stirred up the hope that music was going to save the day, but lately my train of thought was taking all kinds of weird tangents.

> *Perfectly normal. You're grieving for your old buddy. Give yourself a break.*

Visions of playing the Albert Hall would morph into scenes of my own funeral—shot in the neck by a crazed fan, part of the 27 club. Fans and press would surround the church, hoping for a glimpse or a scoop, and for some reason, Jess crying over the casket. That was when I decided weed was a young man's game. I didn't want to think about that. That seemed like a fantasy plucked straight from the past—cheesy and immature.

Clichés are clichés for a reason.

Maybe my stoner days were behind me?

It's all about the dosage.

Dice was a mystery to me. He could be so fascinating to listen to, eccentrically smart and with a pitch-black sense of humour. But at the flip of a switch he'd become angry and depressed, bitterly pointing his finger in every direction like a signpost in the centre of a seaside town, banging on about how he'd change the system if only he could get his foot in the door. One minute he'd be obsessed with the idea of Atlantic calling and all the riches that would come. The next, ranting about how real art isn't about riches, that success can be posthumous, just look at Van Gogh. I felt giddy about the fact I agreed with him on that.

The only thing Dice didn't talk about was what he did for money. It was something shady for sure—strange intermittent hours, lots of frantic phone calls taken in the other room. I don't know how he afforded all the stuff to make the demos with, but he was adding everything up to be reimbursed by me. He'd get angry about the stress of investing so much, blame me for the yelling matches he was having on the phone. He wasn't someone I wanted in my life, but he was letting me off the rent so what could I do? I put up with him because I had to.

How noble.

'Who the fuck is Angela?'

Luckily, Dice was in one of his good moods and said it under his breath, handing me the phone he'd become obsessed with waiting by. Every time it rang was like another lotto ball rolling down the tube, and every time he picked it up, the ball dropped to disappointment—even more so if he had to hand the phone to me. It was usually Jess, on about some fallout between her mates, but on this occasion it was Angela. She'd wanted to make sure we stayed in touch after I got sacked and invited me to the park in Dulwich with her and Archie. I could walk the seven miles to get there—had nothing else to do.

Don't forget your chewing gum, Billy.

I've already said it—Archie was my hero after he told me he wanted to drive a helicopter coz you only had to use one hand. He was as hilarious as his mum and starving for the world, with his bright wide smile, infectious laugh. His confidence around adults was awesome to witness. If you took your eyes off him for more than five seconds, you could guarantee he'd be deep in conversa-

192

tion with someone when you looked back—usually on the subject of tractors. I'd mentioned that I grew up on a farm and that was it, he wanted to know everything! I happily told him what I could remember.

Angela was a single mother fearlessly devoted to raising her son in a world of opportunity. Her family still lived up North, Angela having moved to London to do a psychology degree that got shelved when she accidentally fell pregnant. Graham, the dad, was an absent father, made rare visits and wasn't missed. She didn't talk about him much. It wasn't in her nature to gossip or bad-mouth, regardless of the subject, but basically she'd refused to be the poor begging girlfriend hanging on to his leg as he left. In her eyes it made her more determined to do the right thing by their child—raise him to understand how to deal with whatever shit life throws at you by standing up to it and remaining strong. Archie and Angela came as a package, joined at the proverbial hip. It was a privilege to be around.

After a few hours, we said our goodbyes, vowed we'd see each other again soon and keep in touch. I felt like I existed that afternoon.

Nausea.

Jess called. She'd broken up with Ben, rang me up in tears and asked me to come see her. It would hurt my pockets, but some deeper sense of responsibility told me it was important—like I was an old friend and that's what old friends did.

I can do subtlety.

As she talked me through the break-up, I told myself to listen, to pay attention and care.

> *Give her a chance. Put your mind back on track, reacquaint yourself with desire. It's Jess for fuck's sake.*

I didn't tell Angela I was going to see her when we spoke. I don't know why. I drank a beer on the train to avoid having to answer myself.

> *Jess gave you that same arousing squeeze when you arrived, told you she was pleased to see you, held on to your hands, hazel eyes pretty much screaming 'fuck me' at you. Don't pretend here, man. Don't deny that twitch, just calm down and get a drink in your hand to help you through the day of playing shrink.*

We spent the day in a wine bar surrounded by rugby shirts and sockless feet in Kickers, Jess unloading the details of her break-up and me sinking lager without it touching the sides. I was trying to accept my choice to be there, convince myself it was the right thing to do, push reality away and enjoy myself.

> *She's had a rough time. Brothers all in line to take on the farm, pressured to run the ice-cream parlour, boyfriend a prick, best friend a slut. She needs someone.*

I had much more tolerance than Jess. She was blue-toothed and slurring by seven. I had to hold her back when she started giving shit to some guy on the next table. She thought he was giving me the eyeball when in fact he was just watching the football on a screen behind my head.

Get eyes for Christmas, did you?!

It was pretty funny, and certainly nice to see some of that fire I'd known, but I wanted her to sober up.

'Hey, Jess, shall we go for a walk? It's pretty shit in here anyway.'

She pulled me close so she didn't have to shout, her purple lips glazing my ear. 'Why don't we just walk back to mine?'

There's that twitch again. You did everything right—played the gentleman, steadied her steps, waiting on that tequila for the walk home to slither round your blood and get you pumped. Into her room and she slumped straight onto the bed. Game on!

The walk hadn't sobered her up but I felt straight as an arrow.

Your tolerance is impressive to say the least.

I went to put on some music but her collection was dismal—boy bands and cheesy movie soundtracks.

And?

I sat on the edge of the bed next to her lolled body. I was suddenly thinking about the fight I'd had at school and how I'd found Jess afterwards, the mix of testosterone and adrenaline that sent me running home to have my first wank. How I'd been the first boy in Year 8 to see her topless when I walked into her room without knocking, and how she hadn't batted an eyelid. Everyone wanted Jess at school. Here she was begging for my affections and my reluctance was finally waning. I'd wanted so much for us to end up here. She was my Joan Baez.

Now you're getting it.

I pictured Simon's smug face when Jess snuggled up to him on bonfire night, remembered my fury at never finding the guts to tell Jess how I felt when I had the chance. Maybe things would've been different?

Jess took off her jacket, kicked away her shoes, suddenly breathless in anticipation, like there was one thing left to do before she passed out. She grabbed my face and sucked at my lips, her sticky tongue breaching my puckered mouth. Any doubts I had evaporated and I kissed right back. She pulled me down on top of her, started tugging at my clothes, urging me to rip them off, rubbing her chest with the other hand and picking clumsily at the buttons on her shirt.

Stay cool. Slow things down and put a plan in place. You going down there or not? Face or fingers? When did

you last clip your nails? Do you reckon it's true what
Chris Llewelyn said about making a girl cum just by
rubbing her tits? These are the questions!

I pulled back. She was so drunk she was still smooching
the air where I'd been kissing her. She was fumbling
with her bra, one boob spilling over the top as the wire
twanged and pinched her.

Colin always said that taking a bra off is like roaching
a tightly rolled spliff. Help her out!

I didn't want her to go any further.

Who's gonna judge you?

I looked at sweet Jess, saw past the wayward eyes and
the sordid opportunity to the friend I'd needed so badly
as a boy.
  Two memories collided like planets in the cosmos.

Potatoes in a broth.

I remembered the scene in the Don't Look Back docu-
mentary, when Joan Baez was on tour with Dylan at the
height of his fame and the end of their relationship. In
a taxi moving to conquer the next city, she was eating a
banana and singing It's All Over Now, Baby Blue—one
of her lover's songs. The perfect image of the artist and
the muse—him sheltered in smug sunglasses, gazing
out of the window at the world that was his, her unable

to resist the beauty of the song she must've heard a thousand times.

And then Baez changed the lyrics playfully to incorporate her breakfast.

> *Yonder stands your orphan with his gun*
> *Crying like a banana in the sun*

Dylan turns and tuts. A derisory snarl tells you everything you need to know about the chasm that had grown between them. In that moment he saw himself above Joan's childish ways—looking down, but never back.

And then I remembered the first time I heard Baez's voice, sat at the bottom of the stairs as a child, absorbing distant versions of whatever Dad was escaping to in his study. It was usually men—authoritative and fatherly. Until one day, out of nowhere, her voice filled the walls and all was anew—as beautiful as almond blossom.

Dylan had no right to look down on her. She was human. And so was he.

> *Blasphemy!*

There was no way I was going to take advantage of Jess like this. Even if it meant being a virgin for eternity.

> *Should've had two tequilas! Listen, we need to lose this Joan Baez thing now. Let's call it something else. How about Courtney Love? She looks like she'd have it rough.*

It was clear what I needed to do and I couldn't help but chuckle—I'd been given a lesson in morality by a banana.

'I'm sorry, Jess.'

She graciously wept. I headed out while she slept.

> *No, I'M sorry Jess—technical hitch. Our friend here seems to think there's another path he should be on. Don't stress, he'll be back. He's got this annoying habit of trying to be something he's not. Thinks he can change his spots.*

I came down with a chest infection when I got back from Bath. The bug and no money kept me gladly indoors and away from my vices. I was feeling pretty glum about what had happened with Jess. I hoped she was alright.

Dice was in a permanent funk of green smoke. I actually didn't mind. He was easier to be around when he was stoned—still talking for England, but he slowed down that motor mouth and seemed positive—everything was going to be alright, even if nothing had changed. He was still waiting for Atlantic Records to call. They didn't, and if the tales about the record industry going to sleep for Christmas were true, they weren't going to until next year either.

Dice said he could let me off the rent for now, but I'd need to find some work soon if the record contract took its time to get past the lawyers. He wanted thirty per cent instead of twenty as payback. I smiled and nodded.

He'd finally told me what he did for money. It was some racket he had going moving stolen goods around, keeping the heat off for a family of criminals. That's why we were always up to date with the latest tech but nothing else, and why there could be consequences if there wasn't a big pay-day. He said I might need to do some work for them if things didn't hurry up. I didn't want to get mixed up in that.

I opened up the windows—the wintery city buzzing a dependable minor fifth on the earth's hum. Meet Me in the Morning crackled from the acetate in a jarring E major. In the living area, the beer-crate coffee table was just a collection of tobacco and bottles—bookends to the litter of days gone by. I let Dice do the talking.

'January first. Just like me. I knew you were a Capricorn. I saw it. Recognised the fearlessness.'

I stared at his swollen lids, the spots around his mouth and his seventies David Bowie teeth. I ran my tongue around my own teeth and, annoyingly, Freddie Mercury sprang to mind.

Dice continued.

'Capricorns are courageous. Got a lot of fight. Try telling a Capricorn he can't do something and see what happens! But we need to protect ourselves, man.'

He tapped his temple.

'Protection from the monsters in our minds.'

Inhale.

'And how do we do that?'

Exhale.

'By becoming something else. By being secretive. Wearing many faces—all of them true.'

I mulled it for a minute, dissatisfied with its relevance. I didn't want to be Capricorn anymore. I didn't want to be like Dice.

After all he'd done for you?

Why couldn't I be a Scorpio? Determined, decisive, asser-
tive, resourceful. Interested in the truth and passionate
about loyalty. That sounded good to me. I think Angela's a Scorpio. If not, she should be. I couldn't wait to see
her again. She'd invited me round for Boxing Day and
I wanted to be well when I saw her. I needed a new line
of creativity to keep my mind occupied for the next few
days. I vowed to stay clean for Christmas.

You're like a fucking yo-yo.

In days gone by I'd have strummed my guitar in my room
to keep me busy, but music didn't have the same attrac-
tion it used to. It reminded me of failure. I felt like I'd
emptied myself of ideas and may never write another
song again. Whenever I sat the guitar on my knee, it was
like a leech. I'd have to peel it away before it broke the
skin, and toss it in the corner.

I tried my hand at poetry instead of songs for a while,
but it all seemed a bit dark and I couldn't break away
from the temptation to rhyme everything. My brain
worked in rhythms and I'd always thought poetry was
meant to be free flowing.

> *Truth stays hidden like fruit so forbidden, but the wave
> is still there when it's not being ridden. And some
> lessons won't be understood. Like the ones about trees
> falling out in the wood. God only knows. Only knows
> God.*

I tried writing a novel for about an hour, but that was beyond me. I stared at the blank page, infuriated that I could feel like I had so many ideas, but nowhere to begin. I had a new-found admiration for novelists. To have a vision was easy, but to order it and flesh it out in a coherent thread of tens of thousands of words seemed a remarkable feat. It must take years.

Try short stories.

I remembered being eight or nine, lying on an airbed in the summer house at the bottom of our garden. I remembered midges dancing around a lamp, the smell of wood chippings. I remembered my dad lying next to me telling me ghost stories, his long arm keeping me warm, the excitement of not knowing when he was going to say boo. My favourite ghost story was The Shining. I liked Dad's spooky impression of the twins, and when the janitor gets whacked with an axe, Dad would jump and tickle me so much I could barely breathe. I liked all the stories— Carrie, It, Pet Sematary—and Dad was a great storyteller. Full of theatre. I knew they weren't his stories and that he toned down the horror, so I used to sneak and read passages from the books on his shelf, rifling and hunting down the shocks and thrills. They were complicated and beyond my innocent understanding, and they laid the foundation for me thinking books were hard work that required patience I didn't often have.

Thinking of Dad and his ghost stories, I could see it was probably the drink that animated him. But whether or not he was drunk wasn't important to me then, so why did it matter so much to me now? It's like I'd decided that the good memories didn't count or something?

Well, do they?

That was enough poking around in the past. I had an idea to keep me busy. I could make a kids' book of short stories as a Christmas present for Archie. Creative, time-consuming and nothing at all to do with me. Perfect.

12

THey SAy the DARKEST HouR is RiGHt Before THE DAWN

I agreed with Uncle Paul, Christmas was a waste of time. Although this Christmas I made a wish and it came true—Dice disappeared. Thank you, Santa!

Mum's green eyes crossed my mind. The anger at her betrayal had waned some. Betrayal felt like the wrong word now. Maybe she was trying to protect me all along? Isn't that what mothers do? I thought maybe I should call her or at least send a card with something other than my whereabouts on it, but that was enough dwelling. I needed another distraction that wasn't vice related.

I'd made a kids' book for Archie and something for Angela too. I'd also watched Magnolia at least ten times by now. At three hours and fifteen, it was a satisfying scratch to kill itchy time. The storm of frogs at the end reminded me of the aliens in Slaughterhouse-Five. Something about the lunacy making it all the more real. Perfect sense in a world of illogic.

Another effective distraction was running. It started as necessity when I'd gone out one night to get away from Dice and was freezing my balls off. Just to keep warm I ran, ending up all the way over at the Thames to hear the boats go by. Back in school I'd never had the patience for long distance. I was a dasher in need of immediate results. I'd never had the patience for anything, come to think of it. I was teased and nicknamed Mars Man for a while because of the way I ate a chocolate bar at lunch once, stuffing it in like it was trying to escape—stodgy gak on caramel gums, childishly snuffling for breath. The hard-earned satisfaction of a lengthy jog was a welcome discovery.

On Christmas day I borrowed Dice's sheepskin jacket, thought London would be easier to appreciate while everyone else was indoors. I wanted to see it from a different perspective—I wanted to look up. Past the Imperial War Museum the cannons saluted me on my canter, the brisk wind making my nose run and my lungs like ice packs in a frozen hamster cage. Turning right across Westminster Bridge, the iconic landscape took my panting breath away as I looped around St James's Park and up The Mall for more sightseeing—Trafalgar Square, Covent Garden, Fleet Street—skipping uninterrupted across a real-life monopoly board. I thought about me and Jess running away from the butcher's dog through the lanes of Cornwall as children.

Having left no breadcrumbs, I got Canary Wharf in my horizon, knowing it was somewhere in the vicinity of SE8. I could always see it across the river from my bedroom window, the elite beacon on the top of the pyramid winking at me as I dreamed. I thought about Glastonbury and how I'd do things differently next time.

Turning onto Cromwell's Estate, I picked up the pace for the home stretch, imagined I was racing my long-time rival for the final time before retirement—a fifty–fifty chance of legendary status committed to the history books, or a sad second place, left in the shadow of his victorious competitor. I was winning but I never got to finish the fantasy. It broke as Daubeney Tower lurched into view. It was no home. Not like Angela's.

...

On Boxing Day I forgot my manners, lazing on the sofa as if it were my own. Cosy, terracotta walls and natural wood frames, pictures of Angela and Archie, art inspired by her travels in India.

Archie came in and pounced on me, demanded we play Neddy the Blorsey, where I bounce him on my knee singing the William Tell Overture. It was something my dad did with me as a kid. I remembered it being the most fun a four-year-old could have.

We ate bubble and squeak and Angela poured me a glass of red wine. I apologised and said I didn't drink red wine—wasn't drinking at all actually.

She said she wished she had my control, judging herself as the glass kissed her lips.

It seemed unfair to be making her feel guilty behind what felt like bullshit.

'Go on then,' I said raising my drink.

I sipped it gingerly, portraying the control she believed I had.

Hello. What's going on in here then?

I gave them their presents. For Angela I made a CD of me singing Town with No Cheer. The book I made for Archie was called Percy Woodstump, about a tree that wants to keep its leaves so the birds have somewhere warm for winter.

> *Who's that fella in the pictures over there on the mantelpiece? That Angela's ex? Graham is it? Good-lookin' chap.*

When Archie went to bed, we sat on the sofa, shared a patchwork over our knees, A Christmas Carol on the telly. Scrooge was looking at his own headstone.

Angela wanted to ask me a favour. She spoke softly, almost nervously. I turned away from the ghost of Christmas future, gave her my full attention.

Archie had a doctor's appointment. She wanted someone to go with her.

'Is everything alright?' I asked.

She said it was probably nothing—I could say no, there was no pressure. It was for Archie as much as anything, he really loved me. She looked embarrassed so I reassured her.

'Be supportive for a couple of legends like you? Of course I'll do it.'

> *Nice taste that wine. Make sure you get the name. Be nice to drink it properly some time.*

She hugged me, called me a sweetheart, kissed me straight to the lips. We hid our grins as our eyes locked, then fell to kiss again when Archie came in asking for his mum to come and help him get to sleep.

> *Archie! What a pleasant surprise! Are you fucking kidding me? A four-year-old kid? Your life has only just begun!*

She apologised and said I was welcome to stay.

> *Now they've gone, you might as well neck that wine.*

I downed the wine against my will and slept like a baby on the sofa.

The next morning we lazed around for as long as Archie would let us—watched movies, had a Tom Waits-off. When Angela went and got bacon for the pigs-in-blankets, I pushed Archie on his new bike and spent the rest of the day getting swept up in whatever his colourful little world was pursuing, occasionally flirting with Angela in the few moments he wasn't demanding our attention.

Eventually—albeit knackered—me and Angela got some time alone. We held hands and watched the Life of Brian till we both crashed out on the sofa.

> *The editor will cut this stuff.*

I only went home the next evening because I didn't have any spare clothes and was starting to smell like a student.

Archie's hospital appointment was tomorrow—I wanted to at least appear to be a grown-up.

When we said goodbye, Angela apologised again, said she felt guilty that she was falling for me, that I had my whole life ahead and I shouldn't be spending so much time with someone as old as her.

Well, she's very perceptive. I'll give her that.

I scooped her up and kissed her on the neck, reminding her what a babe she was, telling her I wasn't a kid, I could do what I wanted.

I took a detour run on cloud nine and got into the flat really late, tripping over the mail as I entered. The mail was never mine any more. Only Mum knew where I was and she'd stopped writing ages ago. The shameful pile of unopened letters still festered under my bed.

On top of the mail this time though, was a jiffy bag addressed to 'William The Conqueror'. The return sticker had the Atlantic Records stamp on it, Duncan's name.

This is it!

I hurried to the living area—the best Christmas ever. I picked frantically at the glue and ripped open the envelope, reached inside with jittery fingers, assuming it was essentially a lottery ticket waiting to be cashed in. I pulled out the demos we'd left with Duncan—all three CDs—and a note written in biro on the label's headed paper.

Thankyou for the music
and while I think
you have some talent;
it's not sufficiently
exciting enough for us
at this juncture.

I flipped the paper over, thinking there must be more, shook the envelope like a kid looking for a fiver in a birthday card. There was nothing but disappointment.

Silly you.

It was then I noticed that Dice had been home—his leather jacket dead over the armrest, half a dozen boxes of B&H on the coffee crate, fresh off the boat.

Bullion.

Deflated at the rejection, I pinched a cigarette.

Knock, knock. Open the door, Richard.

Dice suddenly burst in, exhausted like he'd just run twenty-four storeys. He looked skinny as a twig, his voice husky like he'd been yelling for a day straight. He was the last person I wanted to see.

'Forgot my fags,' he panted, eyeballing me for my cig pinching liberties.

Then he spotted the demos and the jiffy bag, gasping for breath. I showed him the rejection note from Duncan. His grey eyeballs rocked from side to side as he read it, about to go into Hulk mode.

'What did I say?'

He scrunched the note in his twiglet fist, threw it down, grabbed the full ashtray and launched it at the telly—fag ash and filters like dirty confetti, and the screen smashed in on itself.

'Fuckin' Nazis!'

He grabbed his fags and bolted gangly from the flat. I tried to ignore everything that had just happened, tried to stay as buoyant as I'd been only hours ago. But my ticket out of the shithole was up in flames and I was living with a madman who was only getting madder.

I chain-smoked out of my bedroom window, fuming at the universe's cruel rollercoaster. I wanted to get Angela back on my mind. She needed me at my best for Archie and the hospital tomorrow.

Canary Wharf winked from a frosty London. Mum's letters festered under my bed. I bet she didn't miss me. I'd never been sufficiently exciting enough.

All great stories start with disappointment. You gonna let a stranger decide your destiny? No, all he's done is get his name in the narrative. Duncan—the man who missed the boat. I'm done with this shit now. The countdown begins.

FiVE!

I overslept and had to sprint the last mile. Angela was waiting patiently at the entrance of the health centre. She had a cute grin when she got nervous. It could make you think she found something amusing—that wasn't the case this time.

I gave her a kiss, but she recoiled, a little disappointed. 'I didn't know you smoked.'

Chewing gum won't hide who you really are.

No one spoke in the waiting room and there was no time signature to the random hacking that sprinkled the hum of strip lights. There were posters about how to diagnose yourself and information on common colds pinned to corkboards on stock-canary walls. I thought about my dad's study—never without music—and the stacks of old medical books that as a kid I'd pretend to read as if they were in a magic library, like The Neverending Story. I tipped a tub of talcum powder over one of them once. It was a great big book about genetics. I was pretending it was an ancient relic that, when I pulled it from the shelf, I had to blow the dust off. Dad wasn't best pleased to say the least, but he found me under my bed later, apologised for shouting and said he wished his mind was as free as mine. I must've only been six or seven. I didn't know what he meant.

Angela was jiggling her knees, checking her watch. I took her hand in mine and squeezed it, wishing I hadn't had the fag that kept me from kissing her.

Archie was playing with the toys in the corner, cross-legged on the carpet with a plastic steering wheel in front of him. He was only using his left hand, his right resting limply on his legs. I'd noticed him on Boxing Day doing a similar thing with his toys and assumed he was practising for his dream job of exerting as little effort as possible. Angela saw it differently. She'd also noticed that his right shoe was more worn out on the front than his left, as if he'd been dragging it while he walked. That was why she'd called the doctor. That was why the doctor had recommended she bring him in to see someone.

They called us through. Archie bounced ahead. Now I could see what Angela was talking about. His right leg was in slow motion compared to his left.

Doctor Carlson was soft and straight, talked Angela through the process. It was very simple, they just wanted to examine Archie's motor skills, get him to walk the room, read from an eye chart, draw a circle with each hand, clap and hop, etc. Angela had a million anxious questions. I figured it best I be the optimistic one and told her that everything was fine, maybe he just had an infection, that I'd cut my knee in the lanes as a kid and the infection spread to the veins, protruding and bright red, making me limp like Archie. Dad had diagnosed it immediately and knew what to prescribe. The infection went away in a couple of days.

Superficial thrombophlebitis?

Dr Carlson was pretty poker-faced, but the grey eyes over the glasses said she didn't agree with me.

'Was your dad a doctor?' asked Archie, cack-handedly hammering a peg into a hole.

'Sure was, mate!'

Dr Carlson pulled her office chair over to Angela, who focused every atom of her attention on the information being delivered. I was trying to listen in, but I had Archie on my knee trying to get me to play Neddy the Blorsey. The doctor was deflecting Angela's questions like a politician on loop.

'At this stage, all we know is that we want to see him again so we can eliminate certain things.'

We nodded.

'Are you the father?' she asked.

I laughed to answer but Angela got there first.

'He's just a friend.'

Ouch. That sting a little?

Outside, the heavens opened—ice-cold sideways rain on film-noir streets. We sheltered under the awning of a newsagent, the headlines trying to sell the millennium like it was game over for humanity. I could see that Angela was worried and I wanted to be able to help. I wasn't bothered that she'd said we were just friends. What, was she supposed to give a detailed history of our relationship? Call me boyfriend? Partner?

Still. Just sayin'.

She didn't need me overthinking everything. I respected her judgement.

It wasn't unreasonable to want a better title than friend.

Angela thanked me for coming along again. Said Archie really loved me.

You hear that? Archie.

'You want me to come and help out? Be with you guys?' I offered, praying for my own selfish reasons as much as anything.

She said it might be best if I don't come by for a bit. She'd told Archie's dad about the doctors and he was arriving tomorrow. He didn't know anyone else in London so would be staying with her.

Good-lookin' guy that Graham.

I deflated, but only on the inside. 'Yeah. I guess. I mean— it's his dad, isn't it?'

She said there was nothing going on, but she had to let him see his boy.

You believe her?

'Will you be in touch though? Will you let me know how it goes?'

She said of course she will.

When is Graham leaving? She still want to hook up on New Year?

'When is Graham leaving? You still want to hook up on New Year?'

She said she didn't know was the honest answer. She was really sorry but had to put Archie first right now.

And Graham a close second?

Archie was hopping in the puddles. Angela put her hand on me, asked if I was okay, asked if I had enough money for the bus. She could lend me some if not.

Pocket money?

I couldn't bear the idea of borrowing from Angela, even if it was only a quid.

Suit yourself.

'It looks like the rain is easing off. I'll be fine. Get Archie home, focus on him. Everything will be fine. Everything *is* fine.'

I kissed her cheek to spare her the stale breath and hoisted Archie up for a cuddle, feeling like the universe had swallowed me whole. Wishing for this ugly phase to pass, I waved them off and started sprinting between shopfronts, trying to tell myself there was nothing wrong—Angela needed some space, Graham was going to go back to Birmingham soon enough. Normality would resume. I just didn't know when.

Normality?

The rain didn't let up for the whole way home. If frogs had started falling, I wouldn't have batted an eyelid.

Four!

Fidget, fidget. Fuck, it's cold in here. Stick the hobs on or something. Hey, you remember going to Ruapehu with school? THAT was fucking cold! Seb snuck a porn into the dorms. Some pretty aggressive gang-banging if I remember rightly. Terrifying! Still I bet the distortion in the long johns of every kid was dirtier than a fuzz box that night. Fidget, fidget. Got to do something with those hands I suppose, eh, Mars Man?

I'd phoned a few places about work but got the same thing from all of them—'Call back in the New Year.' I would, but until then I was like that De La Soul record.

It's just you, yourself and me. Where's Dice at? He'll have the goods.

There was nothing in the way of nourishment in the cupboards—some stuffing mix, dried lasagne, cans of Super Tennents. I was tempted, even though I knew the taste was rotten.

Imagine sinking them.

I wanted to imagine something else.

I didn't hear the key in the door. Dice came straight into the kitchen—didn't pass go—and went directly to the cupboard of pans, pulled out a dented wok, slamming it on the hobs that were already on. He stopped what he was doing and spun in a pirouette of paranoia till he spied me down on my knees where I'd been rummaging in the larder.

'Billy Whizz? Heat costs money you know,' he said, turning off three of the four hobs.

Then he smiled his cat's cunning. 'Glad you're here though—need to talk. I can't keep you afloat anymore, mate. That's it.'

Hear him out.

'I thought you said it was cool for now?'

'It was. Now it isn't. Shit happens,' he snapped. 'Nah, fuck that, holiday is over. You need to start paying me back now.'

I had nothing to come back with, nowhere to turn.

'Here, you can start by helping me with this.'

He pulled a handful of medicine bottles from his jacket. Liquid ketamine.

You said it yourself...medicine.

He was going to cook it all up into powder, then stomp on it with baking soda and sell it in Soho for the millennium.

Enterprise.

As it bubbled away and we counted out the baggies, I was thinking of Hamish and the bombs we used to make, the respect he had for the chemistry. This was very different.

Thirty baggies later and about half the powder was still in the pan, circled by a crusty yellow skin. Dice scooped up a chunk on his finger and raised it at me.

'Might as well hang on to this. You want some?'

His fingernail was dirty. I shook my head and he laughed, scraped the powder from his finger onto the edge of the pan.

Time and a place for that one.

A siren chased the streets around the high-rises outside. Dice slowed to a whisper, a smile like the Joker.

'This is the real shit.'

He slid his fingers into his jeans and pulled out a baggie.

You want to try something spectacular?

It looked like old sherbet. It was heroin.

Latin for heroes.

I thought of Brad Pitt in True Romance—nonchalant with the dope wars going on around him. Vincent Vega in Pulp Fiction—coolly shooting up in his Cadillac on the way to a date with the boss's wife. But then I thought about Trainspotting and the dead baby, Basketball Diaries and the cock-sucking gym teacher, Christiane

F. and—well—Christiane F. I heard the needle and the damage done.

'Nah thanks, man. I'm good.' I gave thanks to the art that shielded me from my own stupidity.

As usual there's work to be done, but it'll be worth the wait when you finally get there. Heaven in a single cell.

Dice didn't care about my answer. He was transfixed on his paraphernalia, thinking about the ritual ahead—foil, lighter and empty biro—as he moved to the chair by the window. Out of curiosity I watched him get smacked from the kitchen. It wasn't like the movies. He didn't look like he was having an orgasm at all—nothing romantic about it.

You shouldn't buy into everything you see in the movies.

It brought out his blemishes, dark scarlet pimples and puppet-string jaw.

You shouldn't buy into everything you see in reality.

I wanted news from Angela. I wanted to know what was happening with Archie and with Graham. The phone had been all too silent.

THRee!

Dice's tin can chugged the streets of Soho as we munched McDonald's—the cost of which had been added to my tab. He was enraged at the stop-starting he was having to navigate—London dressed to the hilt for what lay ahead at the stroke of midnight. I was in the front, unwashed and ragged in smoky threads long out of date with whatever society deemed fashionable. He looked even worse.

What a couple of grungers.

I'd still had no word from Angela.

Graham had probably had an epiphany by now, woken to his missteps and apologised profusely to her, begged her to take him back. She must've seen the light too.

The back of the van was loaded with hot goods—nicked speakers and hi-fis mostly.

The right thing is that Archie has his father back in his life. You can empathise with that can't you? He's probably got him on his shoulders right now, making up for lost time. I bet whatever's up with Archie is serious hospital shit and there's nothing like trauma to bring

about change in a person. Mum and dad back together.
No one wants to interfere with that.

A distant siren. Dice fidgeted with the mirrors and undid
my seatbelt.

'Get in the back. Make sure the boot's locked. And
hide this.'

He threw the bag of ketamine on my lap.

Go on then, get back there!

There was no easy way through the hi-fi mountain. I
slithered into the space between the boxes and the roof,
wriggled along like Andy Dufresne tunnelling through
the Shawshank shit pipe.

I mean—Angela must've loved Graham once. They had
a baby for fuck's sake! Must've had chemistry. Wasn't
he a photographer or something? Didn't they meet in
India? Sounds like an interesting guy. Probably got a
job too.

There must've been a break in the crowds. Dice hit the
gas and we jolted forwards. I slid along the tops of the
speakers and crashed into the gap at the back by the
doors, yelling as I lost my shoe and cracked my head on
the handle.

That was definitely Graham in the pictures. You're
so naive. You told yourself the photos were there for
Archie's benefit. Yeah, right. I'll tell you what they're

there for. They're an ember. There to keep the flame alive. They just have to blow a little—wink, wink.

I couldn't see a thing—trapped like a spaniel in the boot, pawing blindly for my missing shoe. More sirens hooted but I had no idea where they were coming from. Fucking hell!

Graham probably stayed on the sofa the first night. Y' know I bet Angela used Archie as an excuse to get him back into her bed. Probably said it would be weird for Archie to come in and find his dad on the sofa. Yeah, best jump in with her.

Suddenly the van hit a kerb and threw me upwards. The back end swayed as speakers slid to bury me. Dice cursed, swerved the van right, bouncing down off the pavement we must've twatted.

Didn't Angela say they never planned to have kids? You reckon it was a split condom or thoughtless passion? They were students at the time, right? Young and free, only themselves to think about, experimenting, figuring each other out with their lips and fingers, carefree fucking after hours of carefree partying. That could be you. You could have that. Not with Angela though. She's been there. Who knows how many times?

Another siren. This time too close for comfort. I heard Dice yell, felt the vehicle accelerate. We didn't get far, the van suddenly smashing into something outside that threw me into the merchandise. The van halted, the front door flung open and I heard Dice bolt up the street, plod in pursuit. The chase was on out there, the officers barking into their walkie-talkies as they raced past the van.

I wrestled myself from the carnage in the back and unlocked the boot, fell into the streets—a million eyes upon me. I didn't give them my time, just pulled my missing shoe on and aimed for anywhere, fast as I could.

> *Perhaps you should reconsider Jess, you know. Perhaps take inspiration from Angela and Graham and rekindle that thing. Perhaps this, you, here, sprinting in and out of strangers through the streets of an unforgiving London, maybe this is your trauma? Deliverance from disillusionment? Time to change directions, dude—you know which way I'm thinking. Angela doesn't need a fuck-up like you. You want to do what's best for her? Leave her alone.*

If I could find a landmark, I could get myself home no matter how ridiculous the route. I wished I was a crow.

> *Angela's probably out there having a well-deserved orgasm right now.*

TWO!

I took the lift, waved my fob, hurried feet squeaking down the borstal corridor. I slammed myself inside, ready to drop. In the kitchen I threw back pints of water, but I couldn't drink it fast enough—Mars Man on the loose. On the hob, the wok of yellow ketamine winked at me.

Hello.

Wheezing into the living area I tried to slow everything down so I could figure out what the fuck I should do. I thought about packing my things.

What things? Where you going?

I stared at the silent phone—nothing but a paperweight with no hope on the line. Angela hadn't called. I couldn't call her. She didn't need my drama on her plate.

She was busy scratching eternity into Graham's back with her nails. Doesn't bear thinking about. Forget her, man. That's not you.

She was probably having a well-deserved orgasm right now.

Amen.

I wanted to hear someone's voice. Just wanted to know that there was a world outside my own. I thought of calling Mum.

What's she gonna do? She's at the other end of the world getting stuffed by the elf.

I thought about Jess and whether any amount of contrition could rewind the clocks.

Worth a shot. Ooh, hang on—there's some cans in the cupboard. Get them down you before you call. Steady your nerves.

The wok winked at me again as I snatched the Super Tennents from the kitchen. I necked one, but it wasn't enough to numb reality. Who was I kidding?

Well, that's all other options exhausted. Do it!

I stood over the delicious pan of poison.

Horse tranquilliser actually.

One!

I sank my nose into the brown dust and snorted. It stung but I deserved the pain. I thought of nothing except the nirvana I owed myself and the speed at which I could get there. In minutes I'd be high as the tomb tower I had no choice but to call home, wading through utopian treacle, my brain a wad of dough to be kneaded. Elastic legs gave way to dead-weight as I stumbled into the living room—straight from the Ministry of Silly Walks—sank into the chair by the window, accepting my loneliness with a gormless junk smile on my face.

I don't know what I thought about for that hour—no Dice, no Jess, no Angela, not even myself. It was heavenly.

Praise be.

But it didn't last.

Bad chemistry. Dice ain't no Hamish.

I was coming down faster than I wanted—reality nudging for my attention, disturbing my escape. Another line would take that away. Another line would take that away.

Go on then.

That's when I noticed the phone line—extracted and loose from the wall. Dice must've pulled the cord so no one could break his stupor.

Wise. The outside world is bothersome to say the least. Leave it.

I gathered and followed the wire to the end, curiously steering my boggy vision to marry up the socket. As I did it—the phone was ringing!

Leave it!

'William?'
I hung my head like I'd won a marathon and been committed to the history books.
'Angela.'

Full circle.

13

1st JANUARY, 2000.

LONDON, Seg

You've caught me at a good time for sure – eyeing up a leap of faith of all things. The fireworks were amazing.

Off he goes. Riding on a motor bike in the strongest winds perhaps? How unique! That's how you want it to end? Into the sunset? How rosy are those lenses of yours William? The fuck do you see? I see a junky scarecrow in the making that can't open a tin of beans without writing about it. A gump that thinks analysis is next to godliness. Thinks he can change. Thinks he has a choice.

Turns out I do have a choice. To live and not to tell.

Yeah, yeah. Where'd you get that from then eh? Cherry picked from a book you skimmed? We can all do that. And anyway, you can't not listen to yourself. At best you can have a day off. All the while I'm doing press ups in your cerebellum while I wait for the grudge match. I'm embarrassed to have given you so much credit all these years. Not a single achievement you can stand by. Not a single instance of you seeing something through. We can change that, Bill. We can do something that has an ending worth talking about. Something drastic. Not

*kicking a log or shooting a possum. I mean crash and
burn. Two fingers to a world that won't accommodate.
A pale and purple splat on the pavement. A remorse-
less pile of entrails. People think suicide is cowardly.
It always seemed pretty rational to me. Go on. Twenty-four storeys to fall, and none to tell.*

Eh? You're confusing storeys with stories. Is that like that
Lionel Hutz thing? The truth and the truth?

*Stay alone you weasel, it's all you know. Have you ever
been there for anyone? Really been there? Let's look
at your friends shall we? See whether or not anyone
could ever rely on you. This won't take long. Jess? Well,
she hates you. She's invented a new kind of hatred
specifically for you in fact. Then there's Dice, god love
him. He's probably in a cell somewhere. He's probably
getting a sock full of pool balls round his gurning chops
as we speak. Like that kid in Scum. Davis?*

That wasn't Davis you idiot. You don't know anything.
Davis was the poor lad in the greenhouse that couldn't
take it anymore. It was Richards got the sock in the
chops. Courtesy of Carlin, The Daddy.

*Speaking of daddy, let's look at your family situation,
shall we? If we're painting a picture of loneliness.
Mum? She couldn't wait to get rid of you. Guess that
only leaves one person – your dad.*

Hot chili peppers in the blistering sun.

> *Don't forget how little you were there for him. If only his idiot son could've put two and two together. Why didn't you grab him by the scruff in your Oscar moment? Fucking shameful. Absolutely shameful.*

Dust on my face and my cape.

> *He was dying, William, across the drive from you having a wet dream about your best friend. That goes beyond misgivings. That's fucked up, dude. Remember the inconvenience? The resentment at being woken by the drama? Your mum's cries? Now remember how you just stood there while she dragged her husband's gassed up body to the gravel. His long limbs. His blue lips. The ambulance like an open fridge awaiting leftovers. Tell yourself it was shock, but you could've done something heroic, and you blew it. You don't get to choose again.*

Me and Magdalena on the run.

> *You can never tell anyone about that, William. There's no excuse short enough for someone to understand. The world has no time for nuance. It was your fault. Full stop. And only you and me can know it.*

I think this time we shall escape!

That's why no one will ever love you. How could they? They won't know who they're loving. Fuck. I'm good at this, aren't I? Laying out the truth for you in simple terms. I should've been a lawyer. I've got insight. Your only friend. Here to catch you when you fall and believe you when you falter.

Selfish, jealous, bitter, with a devilish talent for deception. You gave but now you only know to take.

You don't know what's around the corner—cold, hard fact I'm afraid.

That's faith, isn't it? Belief in a truth without proof that it's right? I need faith in something real. And to give up the chase.

What chase?

Whichever one I want.

I, me, you, us. Which is which? Getting pretty hard to tell.

I can tell. Anyway, shut the fuck up. I need sleep. I promised I'd show my best side to the world.

What, the world that's waiting to hit you in the face like a shit sandwich in the morning? Ha! Good luck!

Good night.

Don't be thinking you can dream your way through this. You'd better man the barracks for some raging nightmares, boy. The fever's coming.

And if my thought-dreams could be seen.

I'll see you in there of course.

They'd probably put my head in a guillotine.

Always.

But it's alright, Ma, it's life, and life only.

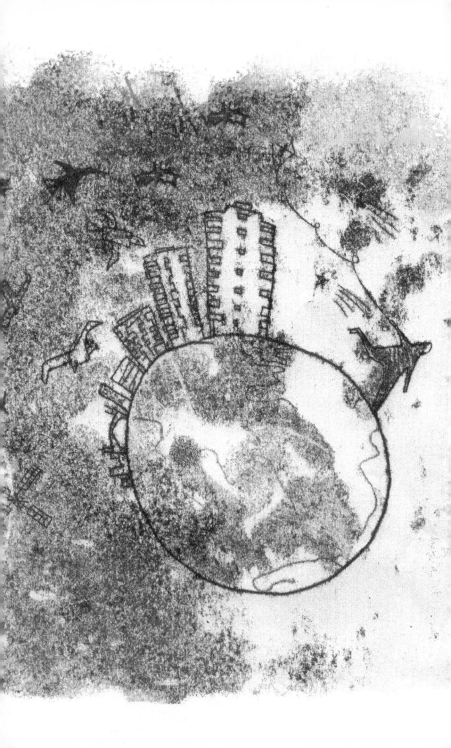

14

Somewhere Between TAKE-OFF AND LANDING

I'm late, running down the streets of a seaside town. It's sunny at the moment but it can turn on a dime. Stag and hen parties are out in force as usual. Lining the pavements with their wigs and wallets.

Sorry. That sounds negative. It wasn't meant that way. I don't know their stories. There are six billion centres of the universe.

...

I'm working in a pub of all places. I went back to nursing for a while, but society pays me more to make people feel ill. The landlord is an angel. The world is full of them. They appear when you least expect and take you as you are. He plays in a jazz band and wants me to learn double bass. Maybe I will. How hard can it be?

...

I wrote a song yesterday called What Price Happiness? I can't decide if it should be major or minor though. I should do one of each and a third that has bits of both. There's no rush.

...

Bump kicked my hand in the cinema. The scan said eighty-two per cent chance it's a girl. It's a love/hate thing with hospitals though. We get as many Yins as Yangs at the moment. Prayers help. And the kid's resilience is inspiration enough to stay buoyant. It's better for us to reflect them than the other way around. I actually quite like my skin head.

...

I dodge familiar traffic towards the pub, grin and greet my boss, who croons my name from the doorway as standard. Sinatra, if I'm not mistaken.

...

It's so smoky in here. I've definitely put on weight since giving up. Bump loves Thai food. We're saving to go to Indonesia when she's born. Mum sent us a music box that plays Chopin when you open the bottom drawer. She doesn't like the name Poppy, but that's okay, I didn't like the book she gave me.

...

A girl with Down's syndrome is eating crisps at the bar. She wants an apple juice and hands me a tenner. She necks it in one and never forgets to use her manners. I haven't seen her in here before.

...

Bill Withers hollers from the jukebox, Sweet Wanomi resting in his arms. Preach it, Bill. To think I missed out on you because of Lovely Day. I was wrong about that. But only slightly.

...

Dad called again and I made the usual excuses. There're still some things I need to iron out. I think I'm trying my best, but my best might not be good enough. He gives me that though. Spiritual allowance or something. I don't give him credit for his actions in the way I should. Good golly, how I wish I could. He has a prayer for every occasion—still looking for the cure.

...

The sun is falling behind three-star hotels. It hits the stained-glass window just right for this time—red lights up, house lights down. A man in a blue raincoat orders a martini.

...

My eyes are open. I only need to think of this.

Acknowledgments

Lines from the following songs are either the title of a chapter or play some other part:

It's Alright Ma (I'm Only Bleeding) – Bob Dylan (© 1965 by Warner Bros. Inc.; renewed 1993 by Special Rider Music)

All I Really Want To Do – Bob Dylan (© 1964 by Warner Bros. Inc.; renewed 1992 by Special Rider Music)

Polly – Nirvana

Most of the Time – Bob Dylan (© 1989 by Special Rider Music)

Knockin' On Heaven's Door – Bob Dylan (© 1973 by Ram's Horn Music; renewed 2001 by Ram's Horn Music)

1979 – Smashing Pumpkins

Oxford Town – Bob Dylan (© 1963 by Warner Bros. Inc.; renewed 1992 by Special Rider Music)

The Lonesome Death of Hattie Carroll – Bob Dylan (© 1964, 1966 by Warner Bros. Inc.; renewed 1992, 1994 by Special Rider Music)

Black – Pearl Jam

Have a Cigar – Pink Floyd

Meet Me In The Morning – Bob Dylan (© 1974 by Ram's Horn Music; renewed 2002 by Ram's Horn Music)

After Midnight – JJ Cale

Heaven Beside You – Alice in Chains

Would? – Alice in Chains

You Sexy Thing – Hot Chocolate

Tremor Christ – Pearl Jam

Visions of Johanna – Bob Dylan (© 1966 by Dwarf Music; renewed 1994 by Dwarf Music)

Avalanche – Leonard Cohen

Diamonds and Rust – Joan Baez

Let's Stay Together – Al Green

Way Down in the Hole – Tom Waits

Between the Bars – Elliott Smith

Pure Morning – Placebo

Open the door, Richard - Louis Jordan

References are also made to lyrics in the following songs by William The Conqueror (written by Ruarri Joseph, published by Blue Raincoat Songs except *published by Blue Raincoat Music Publishing):

In My Dreams
Pedestals
Sunny Is The Style
The Many Faces of a Good Truth
Proud Disturber of the Peace
Cold Ontario
Manawatu
Path of the Crow
Thank Me Later
Bleeding On the Soundtrack
Looking For The Cure
The Curse of Friends
Within Your Spell
The Deep End*
Wake Up*
Suddenly Scared*
Maverick Thinker*